W9-BLO-979

Something suddenly seized him from behind

Bolan was yanked to his feet and the tension in his throat and lower back made it obvious that his attacker was big, muscular and *very* strong. The Executioner tried to twist away from the headlock but his opponent's muscle mass quickly cancelled the idea. Bolan had managed to hold on to his FNC, so he let his feet come off the ground as he rammed the stock between his legs. The grunt of pain was accompanied by a sudden loosening of the hold.

Bolan twisted inward and drove the stock into his opponent's knee a second time. The blow caused the attacker to let go entirely. The Executioner didn't wait to size up his assailant, instead swinging the weapon upward against the man's chin.

Bolan produced the Desert Eagle in one fluid motion, and squeezed the trigger.

MACK BOLAN ®
The Executioner

#245 Virtual Destruction
#246 Blood of the Earth
#247 Black Dawn Rising
#248 Rolling Death
#249 Shadow Target
#250 Warning Shot
#251 Kill Radius
#252 Death Line
#253 Risk Factor
#254 Chill Effect
#255 War Bird
#256 Point of Impact
#257 Precision Play
#258 Target Lock
#259 Nightfire
#260 Dayhunt
#261 Dawnkill
#262 Trigger Point
#263 Skysniper
#264 Iron Fist
#265 Freedom Force
#266 Ultimate Price
#267 Invisible Invader
#268 Shattered Trust
#269 Shifting Shadows
#270 Judgment Day
#271 Cyberhunt
#272 Stealth Striker
#273 UForce
#274 Rogue Target
#275 Crossed Borders
#276 Leviathan
#277 Dirty Mission
#278 Triple Reverse
#279 Fire Wind
#280 Fear Rally
#281 Blood Stone
#282 Jungle Conflict

#283 Ring of Retaliation
#284 Devil's Army
#285 Final Strike
#286 Armageddon Exit
#287 Rogue Warrior
#288 Arctic Blast
#289 Vendetta Force
#290 Pursued
#291 Blood Trade
#292 Savage Game
#293 Death Merchants
#294 Scorpion Rising
#295 Hostile Alliance
#296 Nuclear Game
#297 Deadly Pursuit
#298 Final Play
#299 Dangerous Encounter
#300 Warrior's Requiem
#301 Blast Radius
#302 Shadow Search
#303 Sea of Terror
#304 Soviet Specter
#305 Point Position
#306 Mercy Mission
#307 Hard Pursuit
#308 Into the Fire
#309 Flames of Fury
#310 Killing Heat
#311 Night of the Knives
#312 Death Gamble
#313 Lockdown
#314 Lethal Payload
#315 Agent of Peril
#316 Poison Justice
#317 Hour of Judgment
#318 Code of Resistance
#319 Entry Point
#320 Exit Code

The Executioner

Don Pendleton's®

EXIT CODE

THE CARNIVORE PROJECT 2

A GOLD EAGLE BOOK FROM
W🌐RLDWIDE®

TORONTO • NEW YORK • LONDON
AMSTERDAM • PARIS • SYDNEY • HAMBURG
STOCKHOLM • ATHENS • TOKYO • MILAN
MADRID • WARSAW • BUDAPEST • AUCKLAND

If you purchased this book without a cover you should be aware that this book is stolen property. It was reported as "unsold and destroyed" to the publisher, and neither the author nor the publisher has received any payment for this "stripped book."

First edition July 2005
ISBN 0-373-64320-9

Special thanks and acknowledgment to
Jon Guenther for his contribution to this work.

EXIT CODE

Copyright © 2005 by Worldwide Library.

All rights reserved. Except for use in any review, the reproduction or utilization of this work in whole or in part in any form by any electronic, mechanical or other means, now known or hereafter invented, including xerography, photocopying and recording, or in any information storage or retrieval system, is forbidden without the written permission of the publisher, Worldwide Library, 225 Duncan Mill Road, Don Mills, Ontario, Canada M3B 3K9.

All characters in this book have no existence outside the imagination of the author and have no relation whatsoever to anyone bearing the same name or names. They are not even distantly inspired by any individual known or unknown to the author, and all incidents are pure invention.

® and TM are trademarks of the publisher. Trademarks indicated with ® are registered in the United States Patent and Trademark Office, the Canadian Trade Marks Office and in other countries.

Printed in U.S.A.

We can lose the world, one parcel of real estate after another, while we wait for a shot that may never be fired.

—Admiral Arthur W. Radford
1896–1973

There is nothing wrong with technology when used for the good of all. It is when terrorists pervert that technology to oppress the innocent that I will destroy those who abuse it.

—Mack Bolan

To all personnel everywhere in the armed forces
of the United States of America—
may God protect you as you protect us.

Prologue

Afghanistan

Colonel Umar Abdalrahman stood at the top of a rise and stared at the smoldering ruins of his main operations center nestled in the mountains bordering the Khyber Pass.

His crack team of commandos—handpicked from an elite group among Abdalrahman's various allies throughout the Arab inner circle—had not yet found the remains of his nephew, Sadiq Rhatib. Abdalrahman silently thanked Allah for that. It meant there stood a chance that Rhatib was still alive; if that was true, then he would find his nephew. His men hadn't been able to gain access to the interior of what had once been their main encampment. Whoever had launched the assault against them had used explosives to blast apart the front wooden facade, and this had collapsed the inner structure. The cavernous remains would not be easy to clear, and Abdalrahman wasn't sure he even wished to disturb what was certain to have become a tomb for many of his comrades.

The former mujiahideen warrior turned and studied his surroundings. Bodies were strewed across the neighboring hillside. Abdalrahman stood upon what had served as a helipad. The small attack helicopter they had left there was gone, and there were brass shell casings scattered everywhere.

The bodies along the hillside had been stripped of their equipment.

It looked a lot like the handiwork of nomadic members from radical mujiahideen tribes, but Abdalrahman considered this move a bit too bold. His countrymen were not quite so confrontational; at least, not by their own choosing. They would not have planned such an attack against a numerically and technologically superior force without support.

Abdalrahman thought he knew exactly who had given them that support: the American named Cooper. What concerned Abdalrahman most was that if his nephew were not buried deeper within the confines of the rubble, then he had managed to escape and had gone into hiding, he had fallen into enemy hands. In either case, Abdalrahman wanted to know—he *had* to know. Everything in their plan depended on the safety of his nephew. If Sadiq was dead, it would be significantly detrimental to their plans.

One of Abdalrahman's men approached—his second in command—and reported, "I do not know how much farther we can go without heavy equipment, Colonel."

"Keep digging," Abdalrahman replied with a wave of his hand. "I have neither the time nor the patience to await the arrival of heavy equipment. There were not a lot of explosives used. There has to be a gap somewhere."

The man bowed slightly and walked down the hill to pass on the orders to his men. Abdalrahman looked around him one more time with disgust, and his heart was saddened by the sight. His men had died bravely; he wouldn't have expected anything less. The New Islamic Front would not be scattered to the four winds as other groups had in the past. His men were different; different kinds of soldiers fighting a different kind of war.

Abdalrahman was a practical man, and his mentors and trainers had always touted him as a gifted soldier. He had a leadership ability that was exceeded only by his uncanny skill as a tactician. He hadn't learned to fight the same way as conventional soldiers during his time battling the Soviet invasion of his homeland, neither had he taught his men to fight that way. Abdalrahman believed that the only way to gain victory against your enemy was to fight in a fashion they had never before encountered. Throughout military history—which he'd studied carefully at an underground university in Baghdad during the height of the Gulf War—armies had lost any battle or war where the tactics of the enemy were unlike any ever encountered by that army. The Crusaders had learned this about the Turks, the English about the Indians, and the Americans about the North Vietnamese.

And now, the Westerners were about to learn this about the New Islamic Front. Abdalrahman meant to teach that same lesson to the man named Cooper. And he would do it in such a way that it would never be forgotten. He would write it in the blood of the American people, as it ran into the gutters and streets of some of their greatest cities.

And that was *exactly* where it belonged.

Prologue

Stony Man Farm, Virginia

Mack Bolan rubbed his eyes, yawned and stretched in his chair, his combat hardened sinew and muscles pushing through the torn, dirty blacksuit.

Barbara Price watched him with concern, but he didn't really acknowledge her attention. There was a time and place for more intimate contact, and Bolan knew that Stony Man's mission controller understood that all too well. Besides, Bolan was pretty tired and stiff from his long journey. The Executioner had been unable to do more than doze on the flight from Pakistan, and the coffee he'd consumed had left him no more rejuvenated and with a sour stomach to boot. Even without having to worry about the NIF's terrorist whiz kid—taken into custody at Peshawar and escorted back to the United States by CIA agents—Bolan's job had really only just begun.

The situation still hadn't stabilized such that Bolan could exit and let Stony Man handle the cleanup phase. Sadiq Rhatib was refusing to talk and unless they could get him to start squealing, they stood a snowball's chance in hell of bringing down the roof on *all* of the participants. Still, there were a few players in the game dangling out there, and Bolan was thinking that if he couldn't get Rhatib to roll over, maybe he could get someone else—someone less hardened by religious fanaticism and patriotic fervor—to betray the NIF's real purpose.

One man topped that list. Nicolas Lenzini ran most of the numbers games along the East Coast, and his ties to organized crime were hardly a secret. Anybody who was somebody inside the law-enforcement community knew that it was Lenzini, or one of his immediate Family members, who had control over numbers activities in Washington, D.C. Knowledge wasn't the problem; it was how to get inside the guy's very tight circle of friends. There was only one man who had the kind of experience required for that.

Although he'd kept an eye on things, Bolan had let Lenzini's activities slide, preferring to let the wheels of justice grind away until they got enough solid evidence to put him behind bars. But with the recent intelligence gathered by Stony Man that tied Lenzini and his crew to the New Islamic Front terrorist cell operating inside the United States, it was time to deal with the problem in the only way Bolan knew how: cover, role camouflage and—when the time was right—a full blitz. The rules hadn't changed any since Bolan's first campaign against the Mafia so many years ago, the same campaign that had kicked off his War Everlasting.

Bolan was about to open his mouth and speak to Price when Aaron "The Bear" Kurtzman suddenly wheeled himself through the doorway, immediately followed by Harold Brognola, the Stony Man chief.

The team was gathering to discuss Sadiq Rhatib's campaign for the NIF to seize control of the FBI's Internet packet-sniffer, Carnivore.

"How's it going, Striker?" Brognola asked, an unlit cigar jammed between his teeth.

As the Executioner rose and gripped the man's hand in

greeting, he replied, "I'll let you know after a shower, change of clothes and some shut-eye."

Brognola nodded as he pulled the cigar from his mouth and sat. "I know you need to rest, but I wanted to give you what we know so you can plan your next step."

"I'm all ears," Bolan replied.

"I assume Barb briefed you on the situation with Nicolas Lenzini."

"A bit," Bolan said, looking at Price, "Haven't really had time to get more in-depth on it, but I do think there's enough evidence to assume he's heavily involved with NIF activities here in the States."

"And abroad," Brognola added, not missing a beat. "At least, it would seem that way. I'll let Bear fill you in on that."

As the lights in the War Room dimmed, Kurtzman punched a button on the remote keyboard and the overhead projector mounted into the ceiling displayed the image of a swarthy-looking character in a tailored three-piece suit. The photo image wasn't the best, but Bolan immediately pulled the face from his list of mental files.

"Lenzini?" Bolan asked Kurtzman.

The Stony Man cybernetics expert nodded. "Age sixty-one, place of birth, Boston." Kurtzman looked at Bolan, winked and replied, "A homeboy, Striker."

"I feel so honored," Bolan replied with an expression of mock humility.

Bolan's remark produced smiles from the rest of the team. The Executioner had been born in the war-torn jungles of Vietnam, but his battle on the home front had begun in the small town of Pittsfield, Massachusetts.

"Six years ago, Lenzini started taking an interest in more than just the numbers rackets," Price said. "He began investing in dot-coms all over the place, focusing particularly on the larger ones that provided Web-based services and Internet technologies to anyone requiring them. At first a large number of local law-enforcement agencies were convinced he was just using these companies to launder funds or take bets electronically. Nothing ever came of it though."

"Why?" Bolan asked.

"They couldn't build enough evidence to support a grand jury indictment," Brognola said.

"So they just dropped it," Bolan stated.

"You've got it," Price continued. "After the attacks on the WTC, priorities suddenly shifted. Nobody figured it was worth their time because terrorists were the bigger fish to fry."

Bolan shook his head. "The problem with that kind of thinking is that it doesn't account for the real foundation of organized crime—greed. They obviously didn't figure the syndicate might use that to their advantage, and even go as far as to crawl beneath the sheets with terrorists if it meant easy money."

"True," Price agreed. "And that, coupled with the collapse of dot-coms, left the FBI convinced that Lenzini had simply made a bad investment and lost enough to put to rest any ideas he had about maintaining his legitimate businessman charade."

"But now we think differently?"

"Absolutely," Kurtzman said. He tapped a key and displayed a 3-D map of the United States. The map showed a series of gold stars in various areas of the country, with dotted blue lines connecting those areas.

"Once I got into Lenzini's network, I found quite a few interesting little tidbits."

"Such as?" Bolan asked.

"Well, for one, his system has network-wide security protocols that very much mirror those Rhatib used to cover his tracks inside Carnivore."

"I'd say that's a pretty strong connection," Brognola chimed in.

Bolan nodded.

"Additionally," Kurtzman continued, "he's got an infrastructure as large as the federal information system repositories, and damn near as large as Stony Man's own network. This map shows only the connections within North America, but there are also hits in twenty-seven foreign countries, including a concentration in Europe, and scatterings throughout every remaining continent."

Bolan couldn't refrain from whistling his surprise. "Sounds like Lenzini's been busy."

"What bothers us most is that we didn't catch it before now," Price said. She sighed with a look of frustration.

"I wouldn't get too down on yourselves," Bolan replied. "Not even Stony Man can be everywhere at once. You can't plan for every contingency."

"That's for sure," Brognola added with a grunt.

"No, but we sure as hell can do something about it now," Kurtzman continued. "My team is already working on a new detection program that can head off something like this in the future by allowing us to see it ahead of time. You see, every programmer and technologist has his or her own set of signature work. You could almost compare it to the signature of a bomb maker or arsonist."

"Like a profile?" Brognola asked.

"Sort of, but it's a bit more complicated than that. We *do* build a profile on them, without a doubt, but there are telltale signs they leave behind, and no two are alike. You could call it the electronic version of a fingerprint. Maybe it's the particular system or combination of systems they use to build their infrastructure, maybe it's their methods of programming. Whatever it is, we can hit upon it and expand the profile at an exponential rate. And if we can actually tie this information to the identity of that individual, just like we did with Rhatib, we're one step closer to closing the holes in all of our information and defense systems."

"But for the time being," Price said to Bolan, "we need you to put an end to Lenzini's operations. Basically, we need you to buy Stony Man some time."

Bolan shrugged. "The only way for me to do that is to get a clearer understanding of how Lenzini's work ties to the NIF. What's the motivation here?"

"That's what we don't know," Brognola said, cutting in. "What we can tell you is that Lenzini set up this network to get Rhatib access to specific areas, most of them defensive operational systems and defense networks belonging to the Defense Department."

"Something's wrong here," Price said. "Why would the NIF go after defensive systems? You'd think they would want to get their hands on offensive weaponry, particularly nuclear or chemical."

"That's just what I was thinking as well," Bolan said. "Unless they plan to launch some type of major offensive and use Carnivore to shut down defensive systems. That would render us vulnerable to just about any attack."

"Precisely," Kurtzman added.

"Your friend, Tyra MacEwan, was the one who really helped us to see how this works," Price said. "She possessed key knowledge we didn't have. About four years ago, the Defense Advanced Research Projects Agency started a program called the Next Generation Internet, or NGI, which they nicknamed SuperNet. The funding was sanctioned at the highest levels within the Oval Office and the Pentagon, and plans started immediately for its design, engineering and ultimately its implementation." She smiled and then looked at Kurtzman. "But I'll let Bear get into the technical details."

"MacEwan wasn't real anxious to give up the information

during her debriefing," Kurtzman said. "But I think she trusts you," he said to Bolan.

Bolan nodded in understanding. He couldn't really fault the woman for her reticence. Tyra MacEwan was patriotic, passionate and highly intelligent. Shortly after her appointment to DARPA, she was brought into the FBI on a joint special technology services project to work with Dr. Mitchell Fowler, a respected scientist for the FBI who wasn't the least bit shy about verbalizing his reservations regarding the security of Carnivore. Fowler's death from a sniper's bullet had triggered the events of the past few days, and had nearly cost Bolan, Jack Grimaldi and Tyra MacEwan their lives.

"The concepts behind the NGI are pretty high-level still," Kurtzman continued, "but there are a good number of technologies already in place to support it. First is the idea of multispectral sensors, such as radar and SAR, infrared and microwave. This would be used to increase bandwidth into the multi-TBPS level," he said.

"Could you give that to me again?" Bolan asked.

"Sorry. TBPS is terabytes per second."

Bolan nodded and then waved at him to continue.

"There's also the engineering side of this thing, Striker." Kurtzman tapped a key and the display showed a small, rectangular object—some sort of electronic chip—with a micrometer ruler above it that demonstrated the object was only three-quarters of a millimeter wide and less than one-tenth of a millimeter high. "This is a prototype of a laser array transmitter than can pass transmissions at two hundred gigabytes per second or faster."

"God help us," Brognola said, immediately followed by a sigh that told Bolan he was stunned by Kurtzman's revelation.

Bolan had to admit that he could hardly believe it himself. "Where's the project at right now, Bear?"

"Well, they're telling the Senate appropriations committees that they're a lot farther away from a fully functional system prototype than MacEwan thinks they are. She's not sure why they're hiding this information."

"Okay, let me see if I can piece some of this together," Brognola said. "The NIF recruits Rhatib to break into the DOD's defensive electronic system, using Carnivore as a sort of gateway. The NIF contracts local help from Lenzini, probably for funding and to keep their cells inside the country, while Rhatib starts working the technical angles. And we're exploring the possibility that the NIF has enough inside supporters to utilize this SuperNet program to control our defensive network? Seems a bit ambitious for a small terrorist group. Plus, I can't see us giving them that kind of support."

"I don't think most Americans would, Hal," Bolan said. "But it's possible they're doing it unwittingly."

"What do you mean?" Brognola asked.

"Well, I'd imagine that most of the participants in this SuperNet program are either government contractors or very large corporations conducting business transactions worldwide on a daily basis. Right, Bear?" Bolan looked at the man for confirmation.

Kurtzman nodded emphatically.

"So it only takes one traitor inside a company to turn things around," Bolan said.

"Right," Kurtzman interjected. "All they need to do, really, is provide networking information to an outside source. They can leak enough that any good hacker could take it from there. Plus, Carnivore is virtually undetectable to those security systems. The FBI monitors information constantly across the Internet. It wouldn't be any surprise to see the Carnivore fingerprints on everything. In most cases, companies will be apathetic about this because after all, it's the federal government, and they have to do that to protect us from terrorism. Who's *really* going to question it?"

"Nobody," Bolan said. "And you're right in thinking the NIF's going to use that to their advantage."

"I spoke with the President about the situation before you returned, Striker," Brognola said. "He's refusing to let us simply shut down Carnivore. He thinks now that we have Rhatib in custody, and MacEwan and Bear have things well in hand in closing the remaining security holes in Carnivore, that Lenzini's the biggest threat."

"In this case, I think the Man and I agree," Bolan said, surprised even as he heard the words come out of his own mouth.

Over the years Bolan's alliance with his government had been tedious and shaky at best. Some of the previous occupants of the Oval Office had supported his work, while others used him only when deeming it absolutely necessary. Bolan couldn't deal with the bureaucracies. He was allowed to operate on his own, pursue whatever missions he chose, but he did so on his own and without the support of the very people he worked to protect.

Nonetheless, that deal was okay with Bolan. He wished there could have been a better relationship with his government, but Bolan understood that Uncle Sam had to operate by his rules, just as the warrior had his own. Though the relationship was tense at times, it wasn't unfriendly. And Brognola would lend the support and expertise of any member within Stony Man whenever it was needed. That was enough for the Executioner, and it was actually his preference. He was always cognizant that Brognola pushed the envelope when he rendered assistance on missions outside the approval of the Oval Office, and Bolan was vigilant in insuring that support didn't compromise Stony Man's security.

"Okay, so I've got some idea of where this has gone,"

Bolan said. "Now I need a starting point, and I think we can all agree Nicolas Lenzini is the best candidate."

"We agree," Price replied. "We know that Lenzini's running the operation from Boston, and he's got his two sons handling matters at the other major Internet portals in North America. Bear?"

Kurtzman put the map back on the screen. "Striker, the gold stars you see represent the major network trafficking hubs. They include Boston and Washington, D.C., on the East Block, and out West you've got San Diego, Los Angeles, Oakland, Portland and Seattle."

"Sounds like I'm going to be busy."

"You're not joking," Brognola replied. "We've got less than seventy-two hours to put this thing down."

The Executioner pinned his friend with the icy blue stare and said, "That's a tall order. It's going to take me some time to get inside Lenzini's organization, even if I go right to the source."

"We've already set that up," Price replied. "We have someone inside their system already that will be your contact."

"Leo?" Bolan asked.

Price nodded. "We have word that the guy you shook up when you took down the Garden of Allah nightclub skipped out with quite a bit of Lenzini's cash. His name is Gino Pescia, and word in the OC circles at the Justice Department is that he's gathering up a crew."

"We think when the time's right," Brognola said, "he'll end the relationship between Lenzini and the NIF, carve out a niche for himself and retire."

Bolan shook his head. "Make no mistake this could get ugly real quick. I've been up against the NIF firsthand, and I can tell you that if Pescia tries to pit a bunch of his thugs against them, it'll turn into a bloodbath."

"Lenzini's put an open contract on Pescia's head," Price

continued, "so it shouldn't be hard to get you inside as a gun-for-hire looking for a new place to settle down."

The Executioner could buy that. It was his hit on the Garden of Allah that first turned them onto the fact Nicolas Lenzini was working with NIF. He'd spared the life of Lenzini's errand boy, Pescia—who had blubbered and quivered like a child when confronted by Bolan—and now it sounded as if the guy chose to split off and do things his own way.

Price continued, "We're going to send you in with the Frank Lambretta cover. Thanks to Leo, word on you is that you're known by the nickname Loyal Lambretta."

Brognola added, "The cover story says you got the name working for the Giancarlo Family as a button guy until their collapse in Florida last year. This is your chance to make that rumor a reality."

"And perhaps do a little looking around to see what I can find out about Lenzini's ties with the NIF and just how deep this goes." Bolan nodded. "Perfect."

Price said, "Your recent history is you're just out of Rikers, on a manslaughter beef. That will be confirmed on the inside if anybody checks, and the paperwork is already in place at New York State headquarters. We even opened an arrest record for you."

"Sounds like something I can play with. Not too specific and not too vague. Nice job, Barb."

Price smiled but didn't bask in the moment—that wasn't her style.

"Well, I'd better get cleaned up and catch up on a few winks before I leave," Bolan said, pushing away from the table.

Brognola stood with him and shook his hand. "Sounds like a good idea. You look like hell."

"Thanks," Bolan said.

"Any time. With Jack out of things for a while, we'll have to make some alternate travel arrangements for you."

"That's fine. I imagine once I'm inside that everything else will be on Lenzini's dime."

The Executioner considered the irony of his statement. He'd pose as a tough guy, quickly get on Lenzini's good side, and then topple the Lenzini network and use the old man's money to do it. It was a different enemy now, with different rules, but Bolan knew that the basics hadn't changed at all. They were still ignorant of those within their own ranks and they hadn't been subjected to the skill of the Executioner in some time. Not much had changed in that regard, as far as Bolan was concerned. Yeah, the battle plan was still the same.

Infiltration!
Target Identification!
Confirmation!
Destruction!

2

As Mack Bolan, a.k.a. Frank "Loyal" Lambretta, stepped off the Greyhound bus in downtown Boston, he knew the two men waiting under the overhang weren't the only ones watching him.

He'd spotted the tail in seconds, and his cursory glance marked the guy as a cop. Bolan immediately settled into his role as a tough veteran of the syndicate, just out of Rikers on a manslaughter beef that was beat on a technicality by a slick-boy attorney.

The two men waiting for him weren't hard to spot, either. They were well-dressed, but their suits didn't quite hang on them in a normal way; their clothes hadn't been tailored for fashion but more for practicality. Yeah, they were definitely packing heat. Then there were their stances. To any trained expert how the men watched their surroundings was a dead giveaway. It wasn't just mere curiosity or idle interest—they were looking for trouble, plain and simple.

Bolan ignored the rain that pounded the pavement and rolled off his old Navy pea coat. The Boston weather was a refreshing change to his past two weeks in the dusty climate and mountainous terrain of Pakistan and Afghanistan. The Executioner had been to Boston many times before, but it had been a while since his last visit. And every time he stepped foot in Massachusetts it brought back some haunting memories. But Bolan was concerned only with the situation at hand.

The New Islamic Front had proved itself a formidable enemy in its own right, and Nicolas Lenzini had chosen to ally his family with the NIF for reasons still unknown. That gave Bolan a two-front war to fight, and that was never a good situation for a soldier. His body still ached where he'd pushed himself to the limits of endurance fighting the terrorists and destroying their camp in Afghanistan, but Bolan shoved that from his mind as a minor annoyance. He needed to be on top of things every moment. One misstep around these guys and it would be over. They would immediately suspect something was up and then try to take him when he least expected it.

Stony Man had plenty of intelligence on Nicolas Lenzini's operations, but they didn't have much on the guy's personal life, so he'd have to play any direct interaction with Lenzini by ear. That was okay. He'd played this part many times, and while Bolan *never* made the mistake of underestimating his enemy, he had invented the concept of role camouflage and applied in it ways no other agent who'd ever penetrated the Mob had managed. Most agents either got caught up in the lifestyle, or they just plain got caught.

"You Lambretta?" the shorter of the two men asked.

Bolan nodded. "Are you with Mr. Lenzini?"

As the guy stuck out his hand and Bolan shook it without ceremony, he replied, "Yeah, I'm Serge Grano, the house boss." He jerked his thumb in the direction of his larger companion and added, "This is Alfonse. We just call him Ape. We're the welcoming party."

"I don't think you're the only ones," Bolan replied, flicking his eyes to his left.

Grano turned and looked at Ape. "You know what he's talking about?"

"Nope," Ape replied with a shrug.

Grano looked at Bolan again. "What are you talking about?"

"You guys are being watched," Bolan replied. "By a cop." Grano started to look around, but Bolan immediately stopped him by adding, "Don't look for him or he'll run scared. I'd play cool, wait until he's where we can deal with it."

Grano leveled a hard stare at Bolan. "You're just off the boat, and you think you're calling the shots—"

"I don't mean any disrespect, Mr. Grano," Bolan replied quickly. "But the guy may be watching me, which means he's watching you too, and I don't want to put Mr. Lenzini in any type of a scrape. Okay?"

Grano smiled, obviously pleased by what he was hearing. Part of Bolan's cover included stories of how he'd earned the name "Loyal." He was supposedly fiercely dedicated to his employers.

"Sounds like you live up to your reputation," Grano said. "I think you're going to find that Mr. Lenzini appreciates loyalty. We *all* appreciate it."

"That's good to hear. I'm already feeling like I'm home again," Bolan said. "Now, the only question is how you want to handle this situation, Mr. Grano."

"You any good behind a wheel?" Grano asked.

Bolan nodded.

"All right then," Grano said, turning to his companion. "We'll let him drive, and we can deal with this cop."

Bolan thought furiously. He'd hoped Grano would offer him the opportunity to take the guy out himself—make the new bull prove himself. This was no good. He'd have to act immediately, or there would be trouble.

"We go public with this," Bolan said quickly, "we could have trouble with the cops."

"Are you kidding?" Grano said with a chuckle, clapping Bolan on the shoulder. "We've got half the force in our pocket. We'd be out within the hour."

"Maybe, but I'm not so sure we can afford that kind of attention right now. I'm still pretty hot on the list."

Grano shook his head as he lit a cigarette and then offered one to Bolan, who declined with a shake of his head. "You got a better idea, I'm open to it," he said.

"As a matter of fact, I do," Bolan replied. "I noticed the guy when I got off the bus. Now, if he's here for me and I just walk away, he's going to follow. That proves it's me he's interested in and I can certainly deal with him quietly. If I leave and he stays on you guys, then I'd suggest you go and I'll cover your ass when he's focused on you. Either way, we can meet after at some place of your choosing, with no fuss, no static. *And* we don't draw unnecessary attention to ourselves."

Grano appeared to consider Bolan's plan for a long moment. At first, the Executioner wondered if the guy was going to go for it, but finally Grano let out a chuckle and a gust of smoke. He said, "Yeah, that sounds like a pretty good plan, Loyal. You ever been to Boston before?"

Bolan nodded.

"Good. You meet up with us at a place on Lexington and Ninth, little coffee shop there." Grano handed him a business card that was generic and nondescript. "It's only a few blocks from here. If you get lost, ask directions. We'll wait for you."

Bolan gave another nod then turned and walked purposely past the guy he'd marked as a cop. The man immediately lowered the paper he was pretending to read, turned and fell into step behind Bolan. The Executioner didn't have to see the guy on his tail; his instincts told him he was being followed. Instinct had saved him more times than he cared to count.

The soldier led the cop from the bus station and immediately crossed the street in the direction of a department store. Despite the inclement weather, the streets were full of shoppers.

Bolan got across the sidewalk and immediately hurried into the store's revolving glass door. He turned a hard left and slipped behind a display that didn't expose his back to viewing from the outside but would allow him to reverse roles when his tail came through. He didn't have long to wait.

The man entered and stopped just inside the doorway, causing a woman behind him to stop short and curse him for his unexpected move. The guy appeared to ignore her as the woman stepped around him, gave him the finger and then continued about her business. Bolan focused on his quarry. The man moved away from him and headed toward the escalator.

Bolan followed. The hunter had just become the hunted.

Amarillo, Texas

TYRA MACEWAN SIGHED with relief as she settled into the old-fashioned iron bathtub and let the hot, soapy water work its healing magic on her sore and tired body. It felt good to be home. She felt safe knowing her mother was downstairs. She could hear the woman humming some big-band tune while busying herself preparing dinner. It reminded MacEwan of a more innocent time: a time before the New Islamic Front terrorists and the penetration of Carnivore by Sadiq Rhatib; a time before she'd lost her innocence to the real horrors of terrorism; a time before she'd met a hotshot flyer named Jack and a soldier named Cooper.

MacEwan thought of the two men and smiled. The idea that men like that were keeping people safe was certainly a comfort. With their help, and the help of an electronics genius she knew only as "Bear," MacEwan had managed to avert a world disaster. They weren't out of the woods, not by a long shot. But if anyone could handle the problem, it was the people with whom MacEwan had forged a powerful alliance. MacEwan was especially concerned about Jack. She didn't even know his last name, and it was probably better she didn't, but she'd found herself immediately attracted to the strong, temperamental pilot with the quick wit and the sharp tongue. She knew a large part of Jack's snappy sense of humor and Type A personality had to do with things from his past—things he couldn't, or at least *wouldn't*, talk about. And Cooper was even more closemouthed than his friend. He was a man of unprecedented talent as a soldier and involved in unspeakable brutality. Yes, Matt Cooper definitely had ghosts. Still, MacEwan could see a warmer side to him. It was one that he didn't show much, because he couldn't afford to let down his guard. He lived a life that few could live, and his world was filled with killing and bloodshed and danger. It was the kind of existence that MacEwan surmised would destroy most men in very little time. Then again, she had learned—just in those few short days she'd spent with him—that Cooper was not most men.

There was a sudden but soft rap at the bathroom door, followed by the sound of her mother's voice. "Honey, are you almost finished? Dinner's in fifteen minutes."

"I'll be right down, Mom," MacEwan replied, looking at her watch on the nearby chair and realizing she'd been soaking for more than a half hour. She had to have dozed off because it felt as if she'd just settled into the very hot water that was now only lukewarm.

MacEwan pulled herself carefully from the old tub and stepped onto the carpet. She ran a large, fluffy towel against her firm body. She stopped for a moment in front of the full-length mirror mounted to the back of the bathroom door and studied her shapely curves as she ran the towel against her brown, curly hair.

You're an attractive woman, plain and simple, she thought. Any guy who valued intelligence and sensitivity would think her a great catch.

MacEwan finished drying herself, and after slipping into

jeans, socks and a pressed pink blouse, she headed down the creaking stairs to the kitchen. She found her mother bustling about, preparing dinner in her usual fashion, acting as if there weren't a care in the world. Of course, she didn't have any reason to worry. MacEwan had decided not to tell her mother what had really transpired over the past week or so. Despite the security risks, she saw no reason to worry the poor woman unnecessarily.

Sally MacEwan stopped what she was doing long enough to fix her daughter with an appraising look followed by the approval of a warm smile. She was a short, thin woman with pointed features. MacEwan wondered if she would look like that at fifty-nine. "That's a nice outfit, dear," she said.

MacEwan couldn't help but laugh at her mother's remark, but she immediately stepped forward and gave her a loving peck on the cheek. "I wouldn't exactly call this old thing an outfit, Mom. But I'm glad you like it all the same."

Her mother merely shook her head. "Still just a young smart aleck, aren't you? You got *that* from your daddy. Now make yourself useful, girl, and finish setting the table."

"Yes, ma'am," MacEwan replied. She turned toward the cabinet where the glasses and plates were stored, and her mom swatted her on the behind with a towel before returning her attention to the stove.

As MacEwan retrieved the dinnerware, she looked out the kitchen window into the backyard of the house. The MacEwans had a lot of ranching acreage, the result of years of hard work by MacEwan's father. That same work had sent her to a local university and subsequently to MIT. MacEwan hadn't abused such a privilege, graduating top of her class and going to work almost immediately for the Defense Advanced Research Projects Agency. She'd been with their Information Processing Technology Office for only six months before capturing the attention of Dr. Mitchell Fowler, a genius and the subject of one of MacEwan's college white papers on the security of the Carnivore system. It had been an honor to work with such a distinguished scientist. MacEwan had no idea it would turn into such a deadly proposition.

But she was taking some much needed vacation time and she didn't have to worry about it anymore. At least that's what she had hoped. Her time with Cooper had taught her to look for the unusual in everything, and she was almost positive she had just spotted one of those unusual things. She could see the setting sunlight reflecting off metal.

"Mom?"

"Hmm… Yes, dear?"

"Where are Daddy's binoculars?"

The mother turned to look at her daughter, but MacEwan's eyes were still focused on the metal reflecting light in the distance. She could hear her mother say something, but she couldn't make out the words because of the sudden sound of blood pulsing in her ears. Her heartbeat quickened. Something wasn't right. There were only maybe five or six people who knew where she was, and none of them would have any reason to keep the house under observation.

"Honey?"

"Yes?"

"Did you hear me?"

"No." MacEwan blinked and turned to face her mother. "What did you say?"

"I said they're in the study, bottom drawer of his desk."

"Thanks."

She left the dishes right where they were on the counter, ignoring her mother's inquiries. She went straight to the study and opened in her father's desk drawer. She hated this room every time she entered it. It hadn't been the same since her father had died, and while her mother had tried to preserve things just the way they were, the place had taken on an eerie quality. It was like a damn morgue with her father's strong, vital presence absent. Everything had seemed out of place in the room since his death.

MacEwan shook off the bad vibes, located the binoculars where her mother had told her they were and immediately returned to the kitchen. She brought the device to her eyes and adjusted the focus until she had the source of the reflection in sight. It was a nondescript sedan, coupe-style body, with four men inside. None of them looked like foreigners. In fact, they looked almost like government agents. Still, something wasn't quite right.

"Mom, I need you to do me a favor," she said calmly.

"What's that?" her mother replied as she finished setting the table. "And what on earth are you looking at with those things? It's almost time to eat, and I want to get finished before *Jeopar*—"

"Mom," MacEwan snapped, "I need to borrow your car."

"Right this minute? Why?"

MacEwan spun and faced her mother, trying to maintain her patience. "Because I need to go into town for something."

Her mother made a sweeping gesture toward the table and kitchen cabinets. "We've got everything you need. You did the shopping with me. I—"

"Momma, I'm sorry but I can't explain this right now. I need to borrow the car, and I have to go into town right now."

Sally MacEwan started toward the window, yanking the binoculars from her daughter's hands before she had a chance to stop her. "Are those people you work with watching you? Honestly, you've had a darn heck of a time already. Why don't they leave you alone?"

"Mom, don't." MacEwan grabbed her mother by the arm and took the binoculars from her. "You're right, there *is* someone watching the house, but I don't know who. And I don't want you involved in this. It's bad enough I have to be involved in it."

"In what?" Sally MacEwan asked, stepping forward and cocking her head to one side. "Are you in some kind of trouble? You've been so quiet and secretive since you got in yesterday morning."

MacEwan shook her head emphatically. "No, I'm not in any trouble. But I don't know who these men are, and I need to contact some people who I think could find out."

"Why don't they just leave you alone?" her mother asked again with rapid shake of her head.

"It's not them bothering me, Mom. I have to go. Your keys are in the dish by the door?"

Her mother nodded, following quickly as MacEwan snatched the keys and pulled a light jacket from the closet.

"How long will you be gone?"

"Not long," MacEwan replied, stepping forward and giving her mother a peck on the cheek. As she turned and headed out the garage door, her mother called after her, "Don't dent up that car, young lady!"

"I won't, Momma."

3

Lorenz Trabucco sat in the front passenger seat of the car and slowly pried away the dirt from under his fingernails with a nail file. He hated waiting around, and he still couldn't believe his damned bad luck. He loathed boring-ass assignments, and he sure as hell didn't like Texas. He preferred his hometown of Boston any day of the week.

"I don't know why Serge insists on sending me on these expeditions to shit-kicker land," Trabucco complained to no one in particular. He looked to his wheelman and bodyguard, Lou Maxim, first then looked into the back seat where Mickey "Bronco" Huffman and Joey DeLama sat. The two were dozing off, and at first Trabucco felt like yelling at them to stay alert, but he opted not to. He figured there was no point in being a dick.

Trabucco returned to his manicure as he continued complaining, "It's just that I think I'm beyond this stuff. You know what I mean, Maxi?"

"I know what you mean, boss," the bodyguard replied.

"I shouldn't have to babysit some techno-geek broad, I should be out enforcing." He thumped the dash and then patted his chest for emphasis. "I'm a Trabucco. You know what I'm saying? I come from a long line of enforcers. I don't—"

"Boss, I'm sorry to interrupt you, but it looks like she's leaving."

Trabucco immediately looked in the direction of the house. He could see the car being backed out of the driveway. What he couldn't see was who was in it. "It's too far away. Can't tell if that's her in the car or the old bat who picked her up at the airport. What do you think, Maxi?"

"Looks like her, boss."

"All right, then follow her," Trabucco said. "But you make sure she don't see you. You got that?"

"I got it, boss."

"Hey, you boneheads!" Trabucco shouted at the back-seat pair as Maxim started the car. "Quit your damn loafing and pay attention. The broad's leaving."

"Where's she going, boss?" DeLama mumbled.

"What?" Trabucco said, reaching back and slapping De-Lama's face. "What the fuck do I look like to you, Joey? Do I look like Mumbo Jumbo the Mind Reader to you, or something?"

"No, boss, course not," DeLama stammered, his face visibly reddened by Trabucco's assault.

Trabucco looked at Bronco who was now fully awake and reaching beneath his jacket to check the load in his .45-caliber semiauto pistol. The guy was a strict professional and he loved to kill. The big son-of-a-bitch bruiser—bigger even than Maxim—with his pug nose and shaved head was the only one in the crew that actually intimidated Trabucco just a bit. There were a lot of opinions, mostly conjecture, as to where Huffman had earned the nickname of Bronco, but the widely accepted story was he'd gotten it from the ladies. Supposedly, they loved to ride him like a horse and they insisted he was hung like the same, and that he was a bucking bronco.

Joey DeLama was another story entirely. A young kid who was heir to a Newark crime Family, DeLama had been taken down a few notches because he'd been a big mouth and nearly brought down his entire Family. His father had decided that DeLama needed to go out and get some smarts, so he called his long-time ally, Nicolas Lenzini.

Serge Grano happily agreed to assign DeLama to Trabucco's crew. He was a wet-behind-the-ears snot, too long spoiled by having a father who was one of the most powerful syndicate guys in Jersey, and yet he didn't know shit. In Trabucco's opinion, DeLama was capable of fucking up a wet dream, and the guy had little chance of becoming a made man, never mind heading up the Family business. Trabucco thought it would be better if old man DeLama just killed this spawn he'd sired, and try again.

But that was another story. For now, the important thing was for them to keep up with this government woman. Trabucco didn't know much about her, beyond that; he didn't even know her name.

"You don't need to know her name!" Lenzini had barked at him. "You just need to keep on her ass. I've told you where she's headed, and how to find her. You just make sure you don't lose her, okay? You think you can handle that for me?"

"Yes, Mr. Lenzini," Trabucco had said. "I understand perfectly, Mr. Lenzini. Consider it handled, Mr. Lenzini."

It really jerked his chain that he had to kowtow, but he knew this was his station in life and he had no inkling he'd ever amount to being much more than a bull and at best someday, maybe a head bull. Yeah, maybe eventually he'd get Serge Grano's job. At present, he was subjugated to lifelong service under a miserable half-breed like Lenzini. The old man's father, Marcomo Lenzini, had been of pure Sicilian blood, but he'd never wanted to marry—feeling that his business was definitely a man's business—and instead had chosen to dip his wick in anything that suited him, including one of the young Spanish maids cleaning his house. So in a sense, Nicolas Lenzini was illegitimate, and everyone knew it, but no other woman was able to give Marcomo a son, so he accepted this and made it official by marrying the maid, although they lived separately until Nicolas was born. The old man's marriage proved short-lived; mother and child died during a second pregnancy.

Nicolas Lenzini was raised an only son, and he inherited his father's empire when Marcomo Lenzini—a man among men and respected by all of his associates in *la Cosa Nostra*—died of lung cancer on the eve of his son's eighteenth birthday. So it went, Nicolas Lenzini, barely out of diapers, took over the family business. He became a hard and embittered man, greedy and ruthless with his enemies. He was not temperamental; in fact, Trabucco never recalled Lenzini even raising his voice. Then again, he didn't have to—when Mr. Lenzini talked, everybody listened or they'd wind up fish food in Boston Harbor.

"Where do you think she's going, boss?" Maxim asked.

"Don't know yet," Trabucco replied, "but I'd guess into town. Maybe she's shopping. Maybe she's baking cookies and forgot something. Maybe she's going to a bar to get drunk. Just drive, Maxi. Can you do that? Huh? Can you just drive and quit asking me stupid questions?"

"Sure thing, boss," Maxim replied.

Trabucco knew he was being an asshole, but he didn't care. He was in charge, and he could be anything he wanted. His men didn't take it personally. They were still as loyal to him as ever. What really made him nervous about this whole thing was that what he'd been told about this woman. She was going to be instrumental to Mr. Lenzini's plans, and they were there to insure that nothing bad happened to her. She was insurance, really, against retaliation by the rag heads.

Trabucco still thought *that* was a huge mistake. He couldn't figure out why a guy with Lenzini's clout needed to do business with a group like the NIF. Trabucco didn't trust them, and he didn't want to work with them. But Lenzini insisted that they could all get a lot richer and be a lot better off if they cooperated with them. Trabucco didn't see it that way. He considered the NIF his bitter enemy, just as he considered the cops his enemy, and he wouldn't hesitate to exterminate every one of them if he thought they were going to try to pull a fast one on the Family. This was *his* Family and *his* country, and he didn't give a fuck about the foreigners and what they wanted. He was only doing this out of loyalty to his people.

So he'd sit and watch over this brainy broad and he'd do his job like a professional syndicate bull, and down the line he would hope there was some reward and appreciation for his work. Yeah, and also some damned *consideration.* There was nothing he hated more than when he didn't get any consideration. He didn't care how the rest of the plan fell out as long as Mr. Lenzini was successful. They had to make the boss look good, because when he looked good they looked good, and while he didn't really think that much of Lenzini, the old guy did have a reputation for rewarding loyalty. And so Trabucco knew all he could do was his job. And then maybe, just maybe, he'd get some consideration. Yeah, that sure would be a treat.

Tyra MacEwan parked her mother's car in the lot of a large grocery store and climbed from behind the wheel. She slung her purse over her shoulder, feeling the added but comfortable weight of the .38-caliber Detective's Special she kept in her bag.

She thought about her father as she walked toward the grocery store. He had taught her respect and appreciation for firearms, and given that a group of strange men were following her, she was all the more thankful for his training. She wished she could talk to him about her situation.

MacEwan also wished Jack or Matt Cooper were around. They would know what to do. She knew she could correct that with a single phone call, but she wouldn't be able to do it from the store since the bank of pay phones was visible to the entire parking lot and that might look very suspicious to her followers. Cooper's people had counseled her not to take her cell phone when she returned home, so she couldn't use that, either. The only phone she'd brought was the emergency unit that allowed DARPA personnel to contact her directly, and she didn't want to risk using it.

MacEwan got inside the store and immediately located a manager. A few seconds later, she had directions to the woman's restroom—which she remembered was near a rear exit—and within minutes she was on the back side of the store and crossing a field overgrown with brush, garbage and beer cans.

MacEwan also knew there were an abundance of snakes and rusted metal from junked-out cars in the field. The area had been like this since she was a little girl, and the place really got little attention—except for the Friday and Saturday night police drive-bys—and it seemed the city and public in general had better things to do than worry about this freakish marriage of the natural with the man-made.

After crossing the field unscathed, MacEwan reached a pay phone on the wall of a gas station. She stabbed the buttons mechanically from the number Cooper had given her and ordered that she commit to memory. Within moments a deep, rich voice sounded a greeting in her ears—it was a strong voice.

"Is this Bear?" she asked.

"Yes. Is this who I think it is?" Aaron Kurtzman asked.

"Right," she said. "Listen, I think there could be trouble. I caught someone… Well, several someones, watching the house. Did you or your people order any type of protection?"

"No," Kurtzman replied firmly. "We believe the best way to protect people is not to draw attention to them. That's why you don't have six big dudes in suits and sunglasses walking around you every second."

"Well, then, I could have a problem."

"You recognize any of them?" Kurtzman asked.

"No."

"How long have you been there?"

"Not even two days."

"All right, then go about your business. Whoever it is doesn't plan on harming you."

"How do you know that?"

"Because you'd already be dead," he replied chillingly.

MacEwan nodded at the phone; he was right and she knew it. There was no way she'd still be breathing if those men were supposed to kill her. They could have taken her at any time, especially on her drive into town on the virtually empty road that led from her parents sprawling ranch into the city.

MacEwan trusted Cooper's people, and she knew they were experts in their field. She only had to see the tall, dark-haired, icy-eyed war machine in action one time to know that much. "What are you going to do?" MacEwan asked.

"I'm going to send help. Just sit tight and act normal. I'll have someone at your place within twelve hours," Kurtzman said confidently.

"I understand."

There was a click and the line went dead. MacEwan knew all she could do was wait as Bear had told her. And pray that the promised help came soon.

Boston, Massachusetts

MACK BOLAN DIDN'T HAVE long to wait before he managed to find a nice, private spot in the corner in the menswear area on the second floor. The place was not all that busy; it seemed as if the store catered primarily to a female clientele. The odor of wool, denim and leather permeated everything.

It was simultaneously puzzling and disconcerting to Bolan

that someone could be onto him so quickly. It had been the same during his encounters with the NIF. He'd found Mac-Ewan being tortured and beaten by terrorist thugs, and had subsequently joined the battle against NIF fanatics. Mac-Ewan had worked with Kurtzman in the virtual world to match wits against the technical prowess of Sadiq Rhatib. And Jack Grimaldi had nearly lost his life. Through it all, it seemed like someone was onto him every minute, and he had no explanation as to why. Bolan was hoping this man might have some answers.

The Executioner waited until the man—oblivious to the fact he was being followed in his intense search to find his lost quarry—was aligned with an open dressing room before making his move. He quickly stepped forward, shoved the guy into the dressing room and shut the door behind them. The Beretta was now clear of shoulder leather and Bolan had the man on his knees, the muzzle of the Beretta inches from his forehead. Bolan wasn't surprised to find a gun when he frisked the guy, and he quickly relieved him of the weapon.

"Talk," the Executioner said.

"About what?" the man asked.

"Oh, I don't know," Bolan replied nonchalantly. "How about the first thing that comes to your mind?"

"Well, I'd like to know why you've got a gun to my head," the man said calmly.

Bolan showed him a frosty smile. "Maybe I can tell you that once you explain why you're following me."

"Because I was ordered to."

"By who?"

"By the federal government," the man said.

"Stop playing games with me," Bolan replied, tapping the muzzle against the man's forehead. "The federal government's pretty broad. Get specific or get dead. I don't care which, but decide now."

"All right, all right," the man said, putting up his hands to demonstrate he'd cooperate. "I'm a special investigator with the Defense Department. I was ordered to follow you by Dr. Shurish. You were supposed to report to work more than two weeks ago, and he hasn't heard from you. He was concerned, so he filed a missing persons report with the FBI. When some Washington transit cops spotted you boarding a train for Boston, Shurish called me and asked me to find out where you were going."

Bolan chewed on that for a moment. The story was probably true, although he didn't completely understand it. Malcolm Shurish was head of the Information Processing Technology Office at DARPA. Bolan had first met him while posing as a scientist intended to serve as a temporary replacement until the authorities located MacEwan. Of course, Shurish hadn't known that Bolan was really looking for MacEwan himself. And after the NIF tried to blow him up—and take half the IPTO office with him—he hadn't seen Shurish again.

Shurish's reaction seemed a bit much; Stony Man would have taken care of any questions about Bolan's cover. It didn't sound like the government was looking for him—Kurtzman's systems would have immediately flagged and intercepted anything that came across official channels.

No, Shurish had to be operating on his own. And Mack Bolan wanted to know why.

"Here's my advice to you," Bolan snapped. "I would go back to your own business, disappear, whatever. But don't follow me any more and don't let on you found me."

"You're kidding," the agent interjected with an amused expression. "Right?"

The warrior shook his head. "Just trust me when I tell you we're working for the same side."

"What am I supposed to tell my people?"

"Tell them you lost me. Tell them I gave you the slip, and you think I'm headed for Canada, so they'll start looking for me everywhere but here. That will buy me some time to do what I have to do. And then I'll be out of your life for good."

"You don't honestly think I'm going to go back and lie to my people on your word, just because you've got a gun to my head," the man said.

The Executioner nodded. "Think a minute, man. Do you honestly believe if I wasn't playing for the same team that you'd walk out of here alive?"

The man looked in Bolan's eyes, and he saw two things: the truth was one, death was the other. Bolan could tell it was taking the agent some time to decide if he would buy anything he was being told.

The soldier knew that if he didn't meet with Lenzini's crew soon, it was going to get ugly.

"You've got five seconds left," he said.

"All right," the agent replied. "I believe you."

"And you'll do what I've told you to do?"

"Yeah."

Bolan thought he could trust the man, so he handed back his pistol and stepped out of the dressing room. He looked across the store and immediately spotted a group of security officers led by a man dressed in plain clothes. Probably store security—obviously they had the dressing rooms under some type of surveillance. It was time to find a quick exit, which wouldn't be an easy task under the circumstances. The whole store was probably under closed-circuit coverage.

Yeah, it was time to leave. And the Executioner fully intended to make haste in his exit. As he descended the escalator to the first floor, he realized that the six, dark-skinned men entering the store toting AKSU machine pistols had other ideas. Mack Bolan knew the moment of choice had come: fight or die.

The Executioner reached for his Beretta 93-R.

4

If the new arrivals were expecting trouble, they certainly weren't expecting it to come from above.

The Executioner decided to keep his advantage by leaping over the wide divider between the descending and ascending escalators. As Bolan climbed back toward the second floor, he took the first gunman with two successive shots to the chest. The Beretta's reports were not much louder than muted coughs as the twin 9 mm subsonic rounds punched holes in the guy's torso and tossed him into a display.

Bolan got the second one with a clean shot through the skull before the rest of the crew realized they were taking fire from above. Blood and brain matter splattered across a glass counter, followed a moment later by the gunner's body. The frame collapsed under the weight of the corpse and glass shattered with the impact. The contents of the case—dozens of bottles of cologne and perfume—broke and spilled their odiferous contents onto the counter base and floor, mixing with a rapidly forming pool of blood.

Bolan reached the second floor and started across the room, but he stopped short on seeing the government agent who'd tailed him surrounded by a cluster of security guards. The Executioner ducked between some racks of clothing and weighed his options as the numbers ticked off in his head. It was not likely the gunmen below were part of Lenzini's crew, which left only one likelihood—they were NIF terrorists.

It didn't make any sense, but it didn't much matter because he didn't have the time or luxury to stop and think it through. Without question, the department store security guards were trained to handle shoplifters and riotous customers, but were hardly in a position to handle armed terrorists. Not to mention the chance of innocents getting hurt were a gun battle to ensue between the security officers and NIF gunmen. No, the Executioner would have to handle the terrorists himself.

Bolan made his way back to the escalator. He dropped to his belly and crawled the remaining five feet to the descending stairway. He was betting the NIF crew would be headed up the escalator by now, and most likely they would move in pairs. He lay on his side, waiting until he was about three-quarters of the way down before jumping into view and picking targets. As Bolan suspected, the first pair of gunners were halfway up, crouched on the ascending stairway with their machine pistols held at the ready. The others were positioned to his immediate flank, and also positioned low.

Bolan took them without hesitation, noting that customers were still making for the exits while several employees were clustered around the first two dead gunmen and a manager was screaming into the phone. The Executioner jumped onto the divider, thumbed the selector to 3-round bursts and squeezed the trigger. A trio of 115-grain hollowpoint rounds ripped through the base of one terrorist's skull. The 9 mm bullets nearly decapitated him, and the suddenness of his attack startled the second terrorist. Bolan shot the surprised NIF gunner through the throat, and blood spurted from the terrorist's gaping wounds.

The remaining pair, almost reaching the top of the escalator, turned at the sound of the commotion. The looks on their faces told the story. They had made the worst mistake they could have in any battlefield scenario—they had severely underestimated the ingenuity of their enemy.

Bolan ended the surprised looks with another volley, this one more controlled as the Beretta recoiled in the Weaver's grip had adopted. Both 3-round salvos were true, the first punching through the lungs and stomach of one terrorist who rose and tried to outshoot Bolan. The second terrorist took two of the soldier's shots in his chest and shoulder. He screamed with pain as his finger curled on the trigger of his AKSU and sent a cluster of 7.62 mm bullets into the ceiling above Bolan's head.

The falling debris missed the Executioner entirely, as he was already on the move and headed for the exit. The terrorist threat had been neutralized, and he saw no point in standing around and waiting for a slew of security guards to converge on him. He wouldn't drop the hammer on a cop, whether a sworn peace officer or just a simple security guard. Those men and women had families, and they were simply doing their jobs.

Bolan traded out clips as he left the chaos of the store unmolested. He quickly crossed the street through the logjam of traffic created by the swarm of people reacting to the gun battle. He easily got lost in the crowd. He stopped at a nearby bistro and politely requested use of their bathroom. He splashed cold water onto his face, straightened his clothing and headed for the café where Grano and Ape were supposed to be waiting. Bolan found the coffee shop without much trouble and found the hoods waiting for him, true to Grano's word.

They rose without a word and led him to a back alley where a midsized luxury sedan was waiting for them, engine running under the watchful eyes of a pair of large bulls. Ape climbed behind the wheel, and Grano ordered Bolan to take shotgun. He could feel Grano staring at the back of his head, and he knew the house boss wanted him up front where he could keep an eye on him. Yeah, "Loyal" or not, they didn't trust him—at least not completely.

"So?" Grano asked, once Ape had gotten them out of the downtown area and merged with highway traffic leading toward the Boston suburbs. "What happened?"

"Not much, boss," Bolan replied, trying to immediately settle back into his role. "I don't know who the guy was, but I managed to lose him."

"That right?"

"Yeah."

"You sure you weren't followed?"

Bolan nodded. "I'm sure, Mr. Grano."

"Good." Grano settled back in his seat, and in the reflection of the front windshield Bolan could make out enough of his expression to tell the guy was satisfied. "And you can skip the formalities, Loyal. Call me Serge."

"I'd like to, boss," Bolan replied easily, "but it just doesn't seem natural yet."

"All right," Grano said, slapping Bolan's shoulder. "I guess I can understand that. Let's just give it some time." Then he added, "You're gonna fit right in with us, eh? What do you think, Ape?"

"I think he's pretty square so far," Ape mumbled.

Bolan glanced at Ape's profile a moment, and noticed the guy's eyes hadn't shifted from the road and his fingers were tightening on the steering wheel. Obviously, he thought of Bolan as a threat to his own place in the hierarchy. Bolan had met Ape's kind before. They never went very high in the organization because they were big on brawn, but had little going on upstairs.

These days, mobsters were much more educated than in days gone by; in fact, many of them were college graduates holding a master's degree and even a doctorate. It was a different kind of organized crime, called by the same name but doing its dirty deeds in a very different fashion. New mobsters came from the halls of places like William and Mary, Yale, Harvard and Stanford. They made their mark in the business world, and after they had amassed enough wealth, or reached positions on corporate boards, they struck like the venomous snakes they really were.

Yeah, the days of public hits in the downtown sandwich shops or dumping bodies into rivers were long gone. Now the Mafia controlled much of their business through legal means such as contracts, hostile takeovers, and mergers and acquisitions. Instead of moving their money through backroom laundering operations, they fronted high-dollar investments through pyramid schemes and paper companies. They were like catfish: bottom feeders. They made their move while the political focus shifted to corporate CEOs running once-legitimate companies before letting greed get the better of them. As political action groups and attorneys battled with Senate hearing committees over the ethics of big business, the syndicate continued its activities right under everyone's noses.

As Bolan rode with the mobsters, he planned to insure the Lenzini clan didn't continue operating. They had allied themselves with one of America's greatest enemies, and the Executioner was going to sever the alliance. First he would amputate the hand of organized crime that had soiled itself by an offer of friendship with the New Islamic Front.

Bolan smiled briefly at the irony of it. In some of the Arab countries, when someone stole something, the punishment was to amputate one of the thief's hands, thus teaching him a lesson while simultaneously marking him for life. And that's exactly what Mack Bolan planned to do; the Mafia had stolen from the American people. Once the Executioner had finished marking the Lenzini crime syndicate as thieves, he would turn to their terrorist allies.

Except it wasn't their hands he'd cut off, but their heads.

Washington, D.C.

COLONEL UMAR ABDALRAHMAN arrived in America without fanfare or celebration.

The former Afghanistani guerrilla whose military rank had been an honorarium bestowed upon him by the former Iraqi regime watched his troops take up a perimeter to protect him as he stepped from the yacht.

The transfer from the submarine to the sixty-five-foot yacht had gone off without a hitch. The crew had had a tense but brief run-in with the U.S. Coast Guard, but they quickly lost interest in inspecting the yacht when a call came through from a plane's distress beacon. Abdalrahman was pleased with the decoy his men had created, and the fact he'd made it to American shores with relative ease didn't really surprise him much. Despite the alleged additional precautions taken by the American government to protect themselves from the jihad, it wasn't enough, and it would never be enough. It was a holy war now, and the New Islamic Front would continue to operate within the United States. They were on the brink of making history, and proclaiming victory against America for all of the blood it had shed. In one sense Abdalrahman felt there was justice in the thought that this country and people, whom he hated with every fiber of his being, had given birth to some of Islam's greatest martyrs.

As Abdalrahman moved down the gangplank and stepped onto the dock, careful not to lose his balance on the slippery wood, he caught his first sight of Dr. Malcolm Shurish. He wasn't sure if he was happy to see the man, or if he wished to strangle him. In some ways, he held Shurish personally responsible for the capture of his nephew. In fact, it was Shurish who managed to send word to Abdalrahman and let him know of Sadiq's imprisonment. Abdalrahman had come to America immediately, bringing a crew of his best and most talented soldiers.

Abdalrahman stopped a few feet shy of Shurish, and when he saw the man bow low to him and then step forward and kiss his shoulder in traditional fashion, he let his anger melt away. There was no way Shurish could have stopped the American, Cooper, from going to Afghanistan and destroying everything Abdalrahman had worked so hard to achieve. Then again, he wondered, since Sadiq had been brought to the United States, how much Shurish had done to try to rescue his nephew from the American infidels. Only time would tell.

"It is a pleasure to see you again, Colonel," Shurish said. "I prayed Allah would bring you safely to us, and he has heard me."

"It is good to see you, as well," Abdalrahman lied. "Thank you for sending word so quickly."

"When I heard of Sadiq's whereabouts, I knew you would want to know he was alive."

"Absolutely, and in this you have done right." Abdalrahman began to walk toward the car he noticed was waiting for him. "What of our plans with Carnivore? How soon can we be ready?"

"I am not certain. Sadiq's capture has caused serious delays," Shurish replied, falling into step next to Abdalrahman's quick strides. "I'm trying to decipher copies of his work, but I'm having trouble."

"How much do the Americans know?"

"I can't be sure."

Abdalrahman stopped suddenly, turned and stared into Shurish's equally dark eyes. "For a man with a formal education, who has served on this front as long as you have, you don't seem sure about many things," he said, barely containing his anger.

"I beg your forgiveness, Colonel," Shurish said. "Although I don't believe I have anything to apologize for. As I understand it, even *your* men fell under the tenacity of this man called Cooper."

"Your remarks strike me as seditious and insolent," Abdalrahman said with a warning expression before turning and continuing toward the car.

The silence was heavy until they were seated and riding toward Shurish's suburban home in Arlington, which would serve as a base of operations for Abdalrahman's men until he could decide what their course of action would be.

"I don't mean to be disrespectful," Shurish said quietly, "but I'm sure you can understand my position."

"I'm sure I cannot, so why not explain it to me."

"I've found Cooper," Shurish stated.

Abdalrahman felt an immediate twinge of hope—hope for vengeance. "You have my interest. Go on."

"I had him followed. Somebody in government tried to insert him inside DARPA as a spy. Fortunately, I figured it out and faked an assassination attempt. As it turned out, I believe Dr. Matthew Cooper, who obviously isn't a real scientist—"

"Obviously," Abdalrahman said, interjecting.

"—was looking into Tyra MacEwan's disappearance."

Abdalrahman shook his head with agitation. "Forget the woman for a moment. You said you know where Cooper is."

"He's in Boston. I sent men for him, but as yet I've not heard from them. Very soon, he will either be dead or our prisoner."

"Very good, Shurish. I'm impressed. And what about the woman, MacEwan?" the colonel asked.

"Lenzini has her under surveillance. We must keep her alive."

"Why?"

"I believe she's the only other one who has the technical knowledge required to complete the work if we cannot retrieve Sadiq in a timely manner."

"I'd think it difficult to convince her to help us," Abdalrahman said.

"She can be troublesome," Shurish said, nodding.

"Yes, she has already caused us many problems."

"If there is anyone to blame for Sadiq's capture, it would be her and not me."

"I see. Did it escape notice that it was *you* who was supposed to keep her under control?"

"I tried," Shurish said in protest. "It never occurred to me that she and Fowler would actually discover our work inside Carnivore. I thought allowing her to go work with Fowler would serve as a distraction."

"That is the trouble, Shurish. You think too much and act too little. This is not proper for a soldier of the NIF."

"But as you have succinctly pointed out on numerous occasions, Colonel, I am not a soldier."

"Do not think yourself so clever as to be indispensable, Shurish," Abdalrahman said. "Or so help me, I will cut off your head and grind you into meat for lions. Effective immediately, I am in charge of this operation."

"You have no authority to—"

"I have *every* authority!" Abdalrahman could feel his face flush. "Weeks have gone by. Weeks! What have you done? Can you tell me that? Are our people in place? Has Lenzini finished his work? Are we ready to commence operations?"

"I need Sadiq's help." There was almost a whining tone in Shurish's voice. "You must free him."

"How? Can you tell me? Am I to commit my entire force to freeing him? My nephew is locked up in prison somewhere behind meters of barbed wire, concrete and iron. What would you propose I do? Do you think I'm so deluded that I envision myself just walking into this place and taking him from under their noses? He is guarded by well-armed and well-trained personnel, and I am quite certain the government has determined his value to us. They are no doubt subjecting him to horrors I cannot even imagine."

"Phah!" Shurish countered. "They are civilized in my country."

"Did I just hear you correctly?" Abdalrahman shouted.

Shurish's expression revealed he was thinking very carefully before giving an answer. "While I do not agree with my government, I was born here and that makes me an American. This is my country and my people."

"No, my friend," Abdalrahman replied, forcing himself to stay calm. "You are mistaken. You chose to sell them out to us and for a very hefty price, as I recall. Because you realized that after our first major victory here you would never have the same chances as before. *We* are your country and your people, now, and this is something you should never forget. If you ever say anything like that again, I will kill you. Do you understand me?"

Abdalrahman watched with satisfaction as Shurish squirmed in the seat of the luxury sedan before swallowing hard and nodding. He dropped his gaze, not choosing to look at the terrorist leader. Yes, Shurish was definitely proving himself to be a liability. He wouldn't live forever. He was not loyal to the cause of the jihad, and that meant he couldn't be trusted. But for the moment, Abdalrahman needed Shurish, which meant he'd have to tolerate him.

Once the remainder of his forces had joined him and he'd rescued Sadiq and destroyed Cooper, then he would put an end to Shurish's life. In the meantime, he had more important worries and challenges ahead of him. There would be plenty of time to kill Shurish later.

"For now, we will await word from your men about Cooper," Abdalrahman said, "although I am not confident the news will be good. If they fail to destroy Cooper, then I will deal with him personally. And then we will finish our business with the Americans."

5

Boston, Massachusetts

The home of Nicolas Lenzini was more fortress than residence. Not surprising, considering his enemies.

As he rode up the long, winding drive to the main house, Bolan wondered how they could have gathered so little intelligence on Lenzini over the years. He was both an ominous and infamous figure in the underworld who happened to enjoy quite a bit of time in the public eye, and yet the government had seemed almost inept at bringing him down.

Bolan couldn't criticize them too much. They had to operate within constraints he didn't, follow rules put into place by judges and politicians on Lenzini's payroll, and wade through bureaucratic red tape. They had to have approval for their undercover ops, many times by people who golfed with Lenzini or rubbed elbows in the same social circles. Well, the Executioner didn't have to do any of that, and it was time to bring the numbers king to his knees.

As Bolan got out of the car, he took a quick count of the guards and their positions. Given the size of the grounds, there was no way his initial numbers could represent the entire complement. The guards that weren't visible posed the real threat to him, and given his present count, he believed there were probably quite a few who fell into that category.

"Come on inside," Serge Grano said, motioning for Bolan to follow him. "We're late for our meeting with Mr. Lenzini."

Bolan followed Grano inside, ever conscious that Ape was right behind him and watching his every move. At first they had seemed friendly enough, but as they'd approached Lenzini's estate, he'd noticed a shift in their attitudes toward him. Perhaps they hadn't completely bought his story about the cop who'd followed him, or maybe they were beginning to feel like he'd brought them some unwanted heat. Either way, something had definitely changed and the Executioner knew he was going to have to keep close tabs on the environment.

They seated him in a large, spacious office, and then Grano held out his hand. "Turn it over."

"What?" Bolan asked, feigning confusion.

"Your piece. Nobody does one-on-one with the old man armed. Not even me."

"Oh." The Executioner looked at Grano for a second, making sure to hesitate and show distrust, but then he finally conceded and handed over the Beretta.

"You carrying backup?"

Bolan shook his head.

"Start," Grano said simply, and then he left.

Bolan occupied his time by pulling a small rubber ball from his pocket and squeezing it. It would look like a nervous habit to any spectators, and Bolan was pretty sure he was under scrutiny by hidden cameras. What observers wouldn't know was that it was also therapy for the arm wound he'd sustained while battling the NIF. Those kinds of details had been left out of his role as Frank Lambretta.

A panel in the wall suddenly slid aside and a man in a motorized wheelchair rolled through the opening. His hair was white, and his face wrinkled and marked by all of the signs of age combined with disease. This was definitely *not* the man Bolan had expected to see.

"Good morning, Frankie," the man greeted him cheerily, coming to a stop behind a large cherrywood desk.

Bolan nodded. "I'm, uh—I'm supposed to be meeting Nicolas Lenzini."

"So you are," the man said.

"Yeah. So who are you?"

"Nicolas Lenzini," the man replied.

Bolan shook his head. "No way, pal. This is some kind of joke, right? Like a test of some kind."

The man's laugh was really a cackle, which seemed witchlike under the circumstances. "Oh, I assure you this is no joke, Frankie."

"My name's Frank," Bolan said.

"Your name's what I say it is!" the guy replied. "And I can assure you, I *am* Nicolas Lenzini. You want to know how I can prove I am?"

Bolan nodded, fully playing his dismay at being smacked down.

"Because if I push the button here under my desk, I'll have twenty guys here in five seconds who will yank your smart ass outta that chair, beat you senseless, carve you up with a chain saw and flush parts of you down every public toilet in Boston. Got it?"

"Yeah. I'm sorry. I meant no disrespect."

"I know it. And you're going to find, Frankie, that if you're loyal to me, as your reputation dictates, then I'll be loyal to you. You'll never want for anything while you work for me. You can ask Serge or any of his boys. Now, I know you're a contract guy, but I also know you're out of work and looking for a place to put up your feet. Do this job for me, do it *right*, and you'll have a permanent place to call home."

"That would be nice, Mr. Lenzini," Bolan replied meekly.

"Now, I know you've probably seen pictures of me. And I know you're probably wondering why I look like this and I've got my ass parked in a wheelchair instead of on some hot broad. You wondering that?"

"Yes, actually, I kinda was."

"Well, the answer is it's none of your goddamn business! Okay? You just do what you need to do, worry about yourself, and I'll take of you. My boys can tell you I'm firm but I'm fair. And I only expect to have this conversation once. We see eye to eye with each other now?"

"Yes, sir."

"Good. Now get the fuck out of here." As he spun the chair he added, "Serge will tell you what you need to do."

A moment later, Lenzini exited through the panel almost as quickly as he'd entered. Bolan sat and waited a moment, not sure what to do. He didn't want to look indecisive, but he had to admit he was a bit surprised by the brief and terse encounter. It wasn't what he'd been expecting. But he could understand now why the federal law-enforcement community had had such a difficult time getting Nicolas Lenzini. Bolan's meeting revealed that the man the media called Nicolas Lenzini wasn't *really* Lenzini. The Nicolas Lenzini known to the rest of the world was an impostor.

The Executioner realized the game had changed.

"OLD MAN'S TOUGH, EH?" Serge Grano said, nudging Bolan with an elbow.

No, he's a crippled lunatic, the soldier thought as he nodded. Bolan said, "He told me you'd fill me on the details of my assignment."

"That's the trouble with you guys," Grano said. "You don't learn to relax. You're all business, all of the time."

"The boss said it was important to get this done as soon as possible. I came here to work."

"Young bull wants to prove himself," Grano said, turning to Ape and winking. The men were sitting in a cozy barlike area of the house set aside for the guys when they were off duty. They were eating a lunch consisting of cracked crab, fried okra and buttered noodles. A homemade, chilled, banana cream pie sat on a nearby table waiting for them to dig in.

Bolan had decided to forgo the heavy lunch and instead ordered a turkey club and mineral water. His two criminal associates had looked at him like he was from another planet when he chose to pass on the very generous lunch provided by Lenzini's head chef, but as Grano pointed out, each man was to his own eats like he was to his own women.

"Harry, beat it for a bit, will you?" Grano said.

The bartender nodded and left, along with Ape, leaving the two men to talk alone. Bolan thought it was odd, seeing as Grano hadn't asked Alfonse to leave but he'd somehow managed to let the big guy know the conversation wasn't for anyone else's ears. Once they were alone, Grano immediately got to business.

"It's been a while since Don Lenzini hired outside help for this kind of thing," Grano said in a low voice. He jerked his head in the direction of the door through which Alfonse had exited and said, "In most cases, he uses Ape for stuff like this. And understand it's because Ape's the best at what he does. Nobody's better than him, you got that?"

Bolan nodded and presented Grano with an expression of total understanding.

"But Ape's needed here for something else, and we need somebody who can't be connected with Don Lenzini to handle this."

"So you got me instead."

Grano sat back and nonchalantly splayed his hands. "Why not? Word we get from our friends is that you're the best. You've got no ties to us, only to Palermo in Florida, so even if you got caught whacking someone there'd be no way for the Feds to tie you to Mr. Lenzini."

"Seems smart enough," Bolan said.

"Ought to be," Grano said, studying his fingernails. "I'm the one who thought of it."

Bolan saw Grano for what he was. He was a criminal, but he was the worst kind: he thought he was ten feet tall and bulletproof. Grano belonged to the crowd that always seemed the first to fall when Bolan finally brought down the curtain, and he envisioned in the end it wouldn't be any different this time around.

"So, what's the job?" Bolan asked, playing his part.

"All right, I'll cut the bullshit. The guy you're after is named Gino Pescia. You ever heard of him?"

Bolan thought a moment, unsure if he should give away the fact or not. He knew Pescia was a made man, and he knew he was pretty important from the information he'd gleaned during his encounter with Pescia at the Garden of Allah nightclub in the heart of Washington, D.C. And he knew the club was a front for NIF operations. It was just a smoking ruin, thanks to the Executioner's handiwork. Bolan had told Pescia to return to Lenzini with a message of warning that they should cut their ties with the NIF. Apparently, Pescia had decided it was better to do his own thing rather than let Lenzini handle business in Wonderland.

"I've heard his name in a few circles," Bolan finally replied. "Nothing specific, though. What did he do?"

"That's need-to-know," Grano said. "Just suffice it to say that he's turned on Don Lenzini, and that's not acceptable to the Family. As I'm sure you know."

"Yeah, I get it."

"Now," Grano continued, "we've got a rat that tells us he's holed up in San Francisco and he's getting himself a crew together. We're not sure what he's going to do. Your job is to make sure he doesn't do *anything* and that he keeps his mouth shut."

"I thought Don Lenzini wanted him out of the picture," Bolan replied.

"He does," Grano said, "but not right away. The boss thinks Gino might know some things that are important, so he wants to make sure we get that information first."

"What things?"

Grano smiled and shook his head.

"No, let me guess… Need-to-know."

"Yeah," Grano replied. He looked around and then leaned forward, prompting Bolan to do the same. "We've recently taken on some new business associates. I can't tell you about these guys, but then you don't need to worry about them. All you need to do is find Pescia, and then you sit on him until Mr. Lenzini decides what to do with him. That clear enough for you?"

"Yeah, boss. That's clear."

"Good. Now, there's another thing you should know about, just in case it comes up. You know old man DeLama?"

"Yeah, out of New York," Bolan replied. That was a safe reply, because *everyone* who was anyone knew DeLama.

"Well, Mr. Lenzini's got DeLama's son working with one of our guys and just so you know, the kid ain't real bright. We've got him doing something easy, babysitting some government broad in Texas. Just in case you hear something about it, I didn't want you to be surprised. Keep quiet, do your thing, and I'm sure you won't have nothing to worry about," Grano said smiling.

Bolan nodded, but his mind was working quickly. Lenzini had ties with the NIF, and now he had a crew watching a government woman from Texas. That was too much to cast aside, and Bolan would have to find some way of getting word to Stony Man, since there was little doubt in his mind that Grano could only be talking about Tyra MacEwan.

Yeah, things were about to heat up big time.

Amarillo, Texas

TYRA MACEWAN HADN'T SLEPT well. Following her hasty trip to town, she had returned to her home and tried to act normal. True to Bear's words, nothing much happened.

Someone was having her watched, but obviously they were under instructions not to harm her in any way. MacEwan began to run through the possibilities, but came up empty on everything she thought of. If was her government, Cooper's people would have known about it. If the NIF had found her, she would be dead. If her tails were members of a foreign government, and meant her harm, they would have made their move by now—she'd given them plenty of opportunities.

No, MacEwan was smart enough to realize that the best thing she could do was exactly what Bear had told her to do. She would sit tight and wait for some kind of support to arrive, although as she sat at the kitchen table and played a game with her mother, she had no idea when or how that support would come. She had checked outside, and the house was still being watched by the same crew.

Suddenly, there was a knock at the back door just off the family room. MacEwan looked toward the door, and then at her mother, who was watching her daughter intently from across the table. The older woman raised an eyebrow and studied MacEwan suspiciously.

"Are you expecting company, Momma?" MacEwan asked her mother.

"No," her mother replied, "but I think you are."

"What makes you think that?"

"Call it a mother's intuition," she said, smiling. "I know you too well, Tyra. You've been acting strangely ever since you got back from the store last night, and I think you're trying to protect me. Now is the person at that door friend or foe?"

"I don't know. I'm hoping friend."

"Then you should open it, while I get your daddy's shotgun."

MacEwan nodded and her mother immediately disappeared into the den. She cursed herself, biting her lower lip as she went to her purse, withdrew the .38 and walked to the door. She looked back toward the den, and she could see her mother now standing in the doorway with the shotgun up and held at the ready. MacEwan let her hand relax, holding the pistol just out of sight, and turned toward the door. She took a deep breath and shook off as much of the tension as she could. The door didn't have a peephole, and the ornate glasswork in it sat too high for her to be able to look out. Well, at least it was early daylight, and she'd be able to see whoever it was clearly when she opened the door.

She barely had it open when the first of three men stepped through. He was tall and blond with cold blue eyes. One hand pushed her roughly to one side as the other grabbed the pistol and twisted it from her grip with a blinding and practiced ease MacEwan had never thought possible. The second man through was older looking, with salt-and-pepper hair and muscular arms, and he was immediately followed by a third, who had a pistol in hand and came through the door backward obviously covering their rear.

"All right, you creeps!" Sally MacEwan shouted as she pumped a shell into the chamber. "Let her go or I start shooting. And I'm a pretty good shot!"

The good-looking guy with dark hair and a mustache

laughed as he holstered his pistol. "I'd watch out, Ironman. She might shoot you in the ass just for the hell of it."

"I don't doubt it," the tall blonde said. "But if it's all the same to you, Mrs. MacEwan, we'd prefer if you leave fighting bad guys to us."

He released MacEwan and handed the pistol back to her butt-first. MacEwan took it from him, glanced at each of the men in turn and then wheeled on her mother and put up her hand.

"It's okay, Momma, you can relax. Put away that shotgun." She turned and glanced once more at the blonde. "These are definitely friends."

6

San Francisco, California

As soon as the plane arrived in San Francisco, the Executioner headed for the nearest pay phone. He hadn't wanted to risk a call to Stony Man before leaving Boston, since it was possible Lenzini had him under surveillance. His job for Lenzini was important to the syndicate, for sure, but Bolan still felt like there was some omission in Grano's orders. From where he stood, it didn't seem like Pescia presented much of a threat to Lenzini's operations. That left him feeling like they had sent him on a suicide mission rather than risk one of their own. What was it about honor among thieves? Well, whatever it was, Bolan was pretty sure whoever had coined the phrase hadn't spent any actual time with these animals.

What Bolan couldn't determine were the reasons behind Lenzini teaming up with the New Islamic Front; it didn't make a damn bit of sense and, other than financial security, which Lenzini already had, Bolan didn't see what he stood to gain. No, there had to be something else behind this, and Bolan suspected it was something extraordinary.

Why the whole facade with an impostor, while the real deal hid behind thick concrete and steel—a frail old man in a wheelchair. Bolan knew he couldn't underestimate Lenzini. The guy could sure as hell still plot from that chair, and there was no question he was as brutal and merciless as his reputation warranted. The Executioner figured that Lenzini didn't want to show the NIF that he was a man with weaknesses.

Kurtzman answered on the first ring. "Hey, Striker. How's it going?"

"They sent me to San Fran," Bolan said.

"Ah, the City by the Bay."

"Yeah, his number-two guy sent me here for Pescia, but it's not a hit job, at least not yet. And the guy we all think is Nicolas Lenzini isn't Lenzini at all."

Kurtzman replied to Bolan's explanation by whistling softly. "That's interesting indeed, and definitely some juicy tidbits to add to our files."

"Yeah, he's got a double to stand in for him at all of those public appearances and charity events. But let's keep the information internal for a while. I don't want outside agencies apprised until we know what's really going on."

"Understood. Hal's on now."

"Striker, we've had an incident," Brognola said quickly. "It's about MacEwan."

"What happened?"

"I've put Able Team onto it. Carl just called and says everything's under control. It's nothing serious."

"Not to sound flippant, Hal, but if you had to put Able Team on it I wouldn't say that sounds like 'nothing serious.'"

"We got a call from her last night. Bear had it set up so if she ran into any type of trouble, or if she even *thought* she might have trouble, she could call us. It seems someone's had her under observation."

"Could it be one of our own?" Bolan asked. "You've got a woman who works in a highly sensitive area of DARPA, disappears into a foreign country and then returns suddenly without any explanation. That would certainly put her under suspicion by Homeland Security, not to mention her own people."

"We provided the explanation for her," Brognola reminded him, and Bolan nodded in remembrance that Stony Man had taken care of covering up the reasons for her absence. "After the debrief with us, she was approved for return to work. She elected to take some time off, though. We couldn't very well stop her."

"Well, if it's not our people who are watching her, who is it?" Bolan asked.

"Carl says they haven't had time to find that out yet. They only got there about an hour ago." Brognola chuckled and added, "Guess they almost had quite a fight on their hands. Both women were packing and ready to defend the house to the end."

Bolan smiled. Yeah, that sounded like MacEwan: feisty and spirited and not willing to go down without a fight. "So, what's Carl want to do?"

"He thinks because this crew watching her hasn't made its move that it's not NIF terrorists," Brognola replied.

"Agreed. And if it were a government op, I'm sure you'd know something about it by now." Bolan took a risk and decided to tell Brognola about what Grano had said. "I have a feeling I know who's watching her."

"Who?"

"Lenzini's people, along with some help from the De-Lama Family out of New York City."

"Why would Nicolas Lenzini be interested in tailing MacEwan? For that matter, how would he even know about MacEwan?"

"NIF probably told him. You heard about the trouble in Boston?"

"Yes."

"I was being tailed by someone DARPA sent. It seems MacEwan's boss, Dr. Shurish, sent someone to find me because I was MIA from duty."

"We tidied everything up with that," Brognola said angrily.

"Yeah," Bolan replied. "That's why I think the story he gave this investigator was a bunch of crap. I was a contractor, but it doesn't sound like Shurish had ever mentioned that to the investigator I caught tailing me. The way this guy talked, he thought I was an employee gone AWOL. Now, outside of us, the only other person who knew where MacEwan would be is Shurish."

"Her boss," Brognola interjected.

"Exactly," Bolan replied, "and I don't think Shurish asked that investigator to find me because he was concerned about my safety. I think he wanted to keep tabs on my movements, and report those to the NIF."

"So you think Shurish is working for the NIF?"

"It's entirely possible, Hal. Think about it this way—I'm sure when the NIF got wind that Rhatib was in custody in the U.S., they contacted Lenzini to let him know they were going to come for their sacred cow. After all, they probably need him because he's really the only one who possesses the technical expertise to finish the job."

"And you think they'll come for MacEwan, just as a bonus?"

"Why not? She's their consolation prize if something happened to Rhatib," Bolan said.

"Sounds like maybe we'd better move both of them."

"Yeah, and keep moving them around until I can get things wrapped up here."

"What *is* the story on that end? I caught a whiff of your conversation with Bear…something about San Fran?"

Bolan said, "Yeah. I'm here to find Pescia. It looks like Barb was on the money about this guy. When I had that run-in with him at the Garden of Allah, I didn't get the impression he was much more than a sniveling worm. But apparently he's gathered friends while supervising Lenzini's remote station operations, and now they think he's going to start a full-scale war against the NIF."

"I hope he's not planning to start it in San Francisco," Brognola said.

"I hope that's *exactly* what he does. In fact, I'm counting on it. My plan is to get inside his system and shake him up. Then, I'll turn the tables on him, make him believe I've had a change of heart. I can work the angles much better that way, and it will allow me to give him more reasons for hating the NIF. Whether he or the NIF start this war, I'm going to finish it."

"I know you'll do everything you can to minimize innocent casualties."

"I've got a lot of targets to hit in the next forty-eight hours. I'll do everything I can to minimize the risk, Hal."

"I know," Brognola replied with a sigh. "I guess to ask anything else would be unrealistic. I trust you."

"I appreciate it. For now, I'd suggest you get MacEwan away from home and move Rhatib. I have a feeling the NIF is going to be looking for both of them. I'll contact you again once I'm on the move."

"Good enough."

"Hey, Hal?"

"Yes?"

"Tell Ironman to take it easy. In fact, if he can get Mac-Ewan out of there without them even knowing it, that would be better for me. I don't want to raise suspicions right after Grano told me about their operation in Texas."

"I'll let him know to avoid contact if at all possible."

"Thanks. Out here."

Bolan dropped the receiver into its cradle, then headed for the exit. He'd grab a taxi to the downtown Bay area and start poking around until he found Pescia. He thought he had a pretty good idea where to start looking. Profiles and intel on Pescia were excellent, and Bolan knew the mobster had two weaknesses: girls and more girls. He also had some local jobs moving designer drugs around certain of the wealthier clientele along the Bay. Anybody who knew anything about San Francisco knew exactly where to go for that kind of action, and the Executioner had been to this city more times than he could count.

Yeah, he knew where to start looking. It was time to go to work.

HE WATCHED THE GIRL undulate in front of him, the sheen of her body a combination of oils and sweat radiating under the yellow-red haze of stage lights. Gino Pescia felt a sudden, white-hot throbbing in his pants as he thought of how she'd look in his bed doing *exactly* what she was doing right that moment.

Oh, yeah. He would have enjoyed that immensely.

Pescia turned his attention away from the woman as she started her routine on the pole, and checked all entrances to make sure his men were still in place. His most trusted bodyguard had told him that it wasn't wise for him to be in public, especially since it was likely Nicolas Lenzini had a contract on him. But Pescia had to keep up appearances for his customers.

"The profit I've made from the sniffers and snorters pays my salary *and* yours, so I wouldn't knock it," he'd told the bull. "You just keep your opinions to yourself, and do what I'm paying you to do."

Pescia couldn't believe the nerve of his people. Hadn't he always taken care of them? Sure, he hadn't been around for a while—having to babysit the rag heads for Lenzini all that time in Washington—but he was back now and they were bellyaching. What his people didn't know—because Pescia had decided to keep it to himself—was that Lenzini was a crippled old man who talked tough, but in reality he didn't have any balls. Besides, after the trouble he'd run into in Washington, nearly getting killed by the big creep with the dark hair and the cold blue eyes, he didn't think there was too much more Lenzini could do to him.

Those cold blue eyes…shit. Pescia couldn't even concentrate on the girl anymore. He turned and walked to the back of the club, to a doorway that opened onto a narrow hallway. Lenzini's office was at the end of the hall, with a staircase that led to a second floor. The area was set aside as Pescia's living quarters. Pescia had decided to live above the club, for the convenience and the unobstructed view of the girls—both onstage and in the dressing rooms—through a sweet setup that included sound and video feed. Pescia figured some of them had caught on, because any girls who had complained about his come-ons were usually gone the next day, and those remaining had gotten smart and kept their mouths shut.

Pescia moved through the darkened office, not even bothering to turn on the light. Actually, it seemed a little odd because he hadn't even remembered turning it off last time he walked out. Of course, that had been earlier in the day, and the cleaning staff might have shut it off, although usually they left everything undisturbed. Maybe one of his people had been in there. The door that provided access to the upper floor, however, was ajar and light spilled out of it. Pescia was certain he had *not* left it open.

Just as he reached the door, he realized the fatal mistake he'd made not turning on the lights in the office. There was a click behind him, the unmistakable sound of a safety being released on a pistol. A firm hand gripped his shoulder and the gun was pressed to the back of his neck. Pescia didn't recognize the voice, because the man spoke in a whisper.

"Try something, make a move to run, or even cry out and I'll kill you," the man said.

"What do y-you want?" Pescia stammered.

The man spun him, and even in the darkness the second Pescia saw his face his stomach began to churn. *"You."*

"That's right," the cold-eyed stranger replied. "I can see you didn't take my advice, Gino. You were supposed to take a message back to Don Lenzini. You didn't do it. That's not good. And now I can see you're not as faithful to the cause as you pretended to be. That means your time's up."

"But you…you don't work for Don Lenzini. In fact, you sent me back to warn him."

"It was a setup, Gino. Lenzini needed a fall guy, and you were it. You don't think he'd allow anyone to tie him to a terrorist group, do you? There's a good reason he had you involved in all of his business, running around the country and buying up all those folding companies. You actually think he'd take the fall on that stuff? Why have you do something he was better off doing himself? Why have the body double, and make all of these sham investments? He set you up, and he set up his friends, and now he wants me to finish the job."

"Then go ahead and do it," Pescia said, a lump forming in his throat.

Pescia didn't give a damn anymore. He could see the game was over, and he could tell that this stranger—who had now twice gotten the drop on him—knew it was up as well. He prepared for the guy to point his pistol and squeeze the trigger, thereby ending Pescia's misery as the man suddenly smiled. It was a cold, calculating smile and the guy let out a mirthless laugh before holstering his pistol.

The gunman slapped Pescia on the shoulder. "No, I'm not going to do it," he said.

Pescia was stunned. "What? Are you nuts or something, man?" he asked.

"Pull yourself together, Gino," the guy said, flipping the light switch and dropping into a chair in front of Pescia's desk. "You're too dramatic. Why don't you sit down, so we can chat? After all, it's your place." The man gestured to the big, fancy chair behind the desk. Pescia settled into the chair hesitantly, suspicious of the stranger and never taking his eyes off him.

"Just what the fuck is this all about, eh—?" Pescia started to say.

The guy flipped him a card. "My name's Lambretta, Frank Lambretta. Most just call me Loyal."

"I've heard of you," Pescia replied.

Bolan tossed him a doubtful look.

"Okay," Pescia recanted, "maybe I haven't. But, hey, listen, why cut me the break?"

"Because I know what you're about to do, and so does Lenzini, and I know which horse to back. That's how I've stayed alive all this time. You see, Gino—can I call you Gino?"

Pescia nodded emphatically. Why not? The guy was holding a gun, and Pescia didn't have a piece on him because he should have been safe in his own club. He wasn't going to argue with Lambretta. The dude had already roughed him up once; he wouldn't have been able to take this guy on his best day. Pescia had known early on he wasn't cut out for being an assassin or an enforcer within the ranks, so he'd chosen the business end of the Family instead. He'd tried being tough against Lambretta in their encounter a few weeks earlier. His wounds had pretty much healed, but the scars of shame and embarrassment would always be there. Either way, he'd just been handed his life for a second time; it would have been damn stupid not to listen to what Lambretta had to say.

"Listen up," Bolan said. "Don Lenzini sent me here to sit on you until he decides what to do about this mess. Frankly, I think the old man's full of shit."

"I do too," Pescia said. "I've said it before, man, to my guys here. You can ask any of them."

"I thought I told you to listen," Bolan shot back.

Pescia started to open his mouth, then thought better of it and kept quiet.

"I don't like the fact Don Lenzini's playing footsies with the rags. Moreover, I know you're getting a crew together to take care of business. Don Lenzini knows it too. I respect the old man, but that don't mean what he's doing is right. He's mixing it up with groups we shouldn't trust. He should fight this thing, but he's giving in to them, and I don't know why."

Pescia wanted to respond, but he wasn't sure if Lambretta was finished. This was one rough dude. He wondered if maybe this weren't *another* setup, and he wasn't being tested by Lenzini. But that wouldn't have made much sense. If this Lambretta really was a stand-up guy, and everything he was saying was on the level, then that meant there was a general dissension among the crews about doing business with the Arabs. Pescia saw this as his chance to set things right.

"Now there are only a couple of others who know about this little break I'm cuttin' you," Bolan continued. "Alfonse and Serge are in, as well as some of the bulls, like DeLama's kid and the crew in Texas."

"What crew in Texas?"

"Never mind," Lambretta said. "Guess you don't know about that, so just go on pretending you don't. Important thing here, Gino, is that you take this offer. I'm going to make sure Don Lenzini stays off your back, and you keep on recruiting all the help you can get. Serge wants you to go to every site, and get everything you can. We go alone, the two of us, and we do it alone. None of your bulls can tag along."

"This don't make no sense. Don Lenzini sends you here to off me. Instead, you're going to go against him?" Pescia scratched his head in nervousness combined with befuddlement. "You were just telling me a couple of weeks ago to warn Lenzini to break off with the Arabs. Now, you expect me to believe you're on *my* side?"

"Think about it a moment, Gino. If I wanted to kill you, I could have done it already. I could have walked in here, shot you, and walked out without nobody getting wise about it until they found your cold, dead carcass."

Pescia had to admit that if Lambretta had actually planned to do him in, he would have been fish food by now. The guy had not one but two chances to do him in, and he hadn't. Why have the elaborate setup just to kill him?

"All right," Pescia finally agreed. "When do we leave?"

Mack Bolan's smile was as cool as his reply. "Tonight."

7

Mack Bolan counted it pure fortune that Gino Pescia was even more stupid than he'd hoped.

The Executioner had managed—with ease—to convince the drug runner to rally the troops. Of course, Bolan knew Pescia wasn't doing it out of the goodness of his heart, or even because he felt some loyalty to the syndicate. The guy was doing it to save his own skin; Bolan didn't really care what Pescia's reasons were. It appeared he'd maneuvered Pescia where he wanted him, and when the time was right, he'd destroy the guy.

In the meantime he had some business to attend to before he'd meet Pescia at the hotel room Bolan had secured under the Lambretta cover. It hadn't been difficult for him to get Pescia bragging about how he'd already acquired a crew of about twenty-five guns. Pescia let it out that those men were holed up in a deserted motel on the edge of the city. Bolan planned to conclude his business with that crew this night, but first things first. He needed to get in touch with Grano and plant some seeds.

Bolan dialed Serge Grano's number and waited three rings before hanging up. Then he called the second number Grano had given him, and the head bull picked up on the first ring. It had been their arranged signal to indicate Bolan had found their little package.

"You work quick," Grano said. The words seemed sarcastic, but the tone was good-natured enough. "The boss is going to be pleased."

"I followed the stink," Bolan replied.

"Where's he at?"

"He's staying above some club he's got out here called the Twin Rockets."

"Yeah, that's a titty bar he owns with some other bastard. The boss told Gino that if he wanted to keep that place open, he'd have to work with the local bosses there. Obviously, he's still operating on his own. The boss ain't going to be happy to hear that."

"Well, I know where he is now. What do you want me to do with him?"

"Just as we discussed," Grano said. "Don't do nothing until we can figure out what the guy knows. Have you made contact yet?"

Bolan thought furiously for a moment, trying to decide if he should lie, but he quickly decided against it. The truth—or as close to it as possible—was always best, because there were eyes and ears everywhere. If he was seen by one of Grano's informants, and he lied about it, he'd lose their trust. He had to believe that he wasn't the only one out here working for Lenzini, and there was every chance he was being tested to see if he'd live up to his namesake. Naturally, Bolan would have to wipe out any observers before he connected again with Pescia, but he didn't think that would be too much of a problem.

"Yeah, we talked," Bolan said. "I told him that for now he ought to watch himself and that the boss wanted to talk with him."

"What did he say?"

"He didn't seem too thrilled. He says he split because he ran into some guy working for the Feds at a place called the Garden of Ali, or something?"

"It's not Ali, it's—" Grano began, but he apparently thought better of it and shut up. Bolan nodded as Grano continued, "Never mind that, it ain't important. Just keep your eye on him. You've done a good job so far. I'll make sure the boss gets wind of it. Sit tight and wait to hear from me."

"Fine." Bolan didn't hang up until he heard the click of the receiver.

This was immediately followed by the click of the lock to his hotel door. Somebody had picked it, and the Executioner had to believe whoever was coming through had an agenda that included assassination. Bolan took a flying leap and rolled across the bed as the door swung quickly inward. He landed in a crouch on the far side, the Beretta in his grasp and tracking on the door. Four guys burst through it—big muscular types in business suits—one pair toting machine pistols while the two leading the charge had semiautomatics drawn and ready.

Bolan was also ready, and it seemed apparent that his would-be assailants weren't prepared for such a swift and deadly response. Bolan set the selector to 3-round bursts and squeezed the trigger. The first trio of 9 mm Parabellum rounds caught the biggest of the quartet in the chest. Blood spewed from his mouth as the rounds punctured his lungs. The gunman's body twisted in an arc and he crashed against the wall.

The Executioner rolled away from his spot as the pair with SMGs opened up on his position. Bolan immediately recognized the unmistakable chatter of the weapons: Uzis. He planned to avoid becoming a victim of the precision weapon, and he found salvation in the duffel bag that brushed his foot as he rolled away from the assault. The Executioner reached into the sack as he raised the pistol and fired another 3-round burst intended to keep heads down more than to really hit anything. A moment later, the warrior managed to draw a new messenger of death into the fray.

The Fabrique Nationale FNC had become a favorite of the Executioner's for its power and versatility. While considered an automatic rifle of carbine origin, the weapon was built upon the success of the 7.26 mm FAL. The FNC had a collapsible stock, which provided the compact frame of an SMG, but it provided a 30-round detachable box magazine and chambered the popular 5.56 .45 mm NATO rounds. He had already prepared and loaded the weapon in anticipation of his assault on Pescia's crew, so it was ready to do business with these new arrivals.

Bolan steadied the FNC on the table with his left hand, brought the weapon into battery and triggered a full-auto burn. His ears rang as the FNC chugged angrily, the targets falling under a merciless onslaught of high-velocity rounds. A horizontal line of bullets caught one in the stomach, effectively disemboweling him before tossing his body against a wall. Another hail of slugs caught the other submachine-gunner in the head, splitting his skull and splattering the immediate area with blood and brain matter. The last one fell under shots to pelvis, hips and chest. He stood erect for a moment, then dropped his pistol and teetered on wobbly, shattered limbs before falling to the carpet with a dull thud.

Bolan rose in the aftermath of the destruction, smoke wafting from the muzzle of the FNC. He holstered his Beretta and dropped the FNC into the bag. He searched the bodies quickly, relieved them of their identification—even if they were probably fake—then collected everything personal from the room except one piece of evidence that would identify him as Frank Lambretta. Word would get back to Serge Grano soon enough. When the guy heard there had been trouble, and there was no word from Bolan, he and Ape would beat feet out here and try to do damage control.

It was time for a hasty exit. The police would be arriving quickly, and Bolan didn't want to be around when they got there. He had a lot to do, and he couldn't afford any sort of delay or entanglement with the local law enforcement. The numbers were running down.

Bolan found a back exit from the hotel and a short walk later, he was in his car and headed toward the motel where Pescia's people were supposedly awaiting their chance to deal a crippling blow to the NIF. Bolan knew the key to making his plan work was ensuring Lenzini thought the NIF had made the first move. Conversely, he had to convince the NIF that it was Lenzini who had betrayed them, and he knew Pescia was going to provide the key to that. It was a game of cat-and-mouse, one for which Bolan was uniquely skilled.

Nothing had changed in his war plan—just in the players.

It took him about forty-five minutes to get to his destination. Pescia bragged that from the outside the motel looked deserted, but he'd used money from the club to perform secret renovations. It had running water, electricity, and even satellite television to keep the boys entertained. The motel occupied a few acres near a publicly maintained forest preserve off a nondescript exit. The motel wasn't even visible from the highway, and the signs that had once announced of its presence were long gone. A roving guard kept an eye on things and made sure nobody got too close or too nosy. Not that they had to even worry about such a thing, since to anyone who lived in the area knew the place had been abandoned for years, and parents cautioned children from playing near it for fear of hurting themselves. It was the perfect place to keep a large number of men until you were ready to use them. The Executioner intended to make sure that never happened.

When Bolan reached the road leading to the motel, he killed the rental's headlights. The soldier pulled behind some brush and parked the rental beyond the wood line where he wouldn't be detected. The woods were eerie and black, and as Bolan climbed from the vehicle he heard the call of an owl from a nearby tree. The Executioner brought the weapons bag from the car, and moved to the trunk to obtain the rest of his equipment.

Bolan quickly changed into his blacksuit and slipped on a load-bearing equipment harness. He attached a series of standard fragmentation as well as specialized grenades to the straps, and four full magazines for the FNC to his belt. He also slid a Colt Combat Commander knife into the quick-release sheath attached to the straps, which held the knife in place with the handle down. He dropped the .44 Magnum Desert Eagle into a holster on his right hip to complete his war ensemble. He decided to leave the Beretta under the front seat of the car.

Bolan donned night-vision goggles and began his journey through the woods. It didn't make sense why Pescia would hide his crew like this. The Executioner had considered it entirely possible that the mobster had only told Bolan about the place as a stall tactic until he could send the ambush team, but the soldier didn't have any proof of this. That seemed like a pretty big risk to take, not to mention that the story seemed a bit too detailed and elaborate for Pescia to have come up with on a whim. The mobster wasn't that bright. It also assumed that Bolan's visitors had come from Pescia.

Lenzini and his people were the only others who knew where he was staying, but that didn't make sense either. Why would they have sent him here and tried to kill him before they even knew he'd found Pescia? The Executioner's would-be assassins hadn't come from the NIF, of this much he was certain, so that left someone inside Lenzini's crew. Bolan would find out soon enough.

Bolan reached the wood line that bordered the motel. It was difficult to see much even through the googles, since the sky was overcast and what starlight that was visible was obscured by the woods. Still, it was enough for Bolan to make out the sentries walking around the perimeter of the motel: it looked like Pescia had told him the truth after all.

The Executioner stripped off the goggles, put them back in his weapons bag, and brought the FNC up and into a ready position. Given the fact this would be a night operation, Bolan had outfitted the weapon with a special infrared scope with a thermal sleeve that prevented the heat from the barrel from interfering with the infrared signature.

Bolan pressed the rubber cup of the sight to his eye and continued his reconnaissance of the area. After five minutes, he determined there were three sentries in total, two roving and one stationary at the office door. Each one appeared armed with an automatic rifle that, from its shape, Bolan guessed was an M-16. The FNC wasn't sound suppressed, which meant he had to take all three within the span of no more than five seconds, and he'd probably get another ten to cross the distance from the wood line to the building before those inside could react. It wasn't much.

Either way, the Executioner had learned to play the cards he was dealt.

Bolan waited until both roving sentries were visible, then sighted on the one farthest, since he would have the best chance for finding quick cover when the shooting started. Bolan set the selector switch to single shots…took a breath…let out half…

Bang!

The reaction of the first target wasn't visible as Bolan, his eye never leaving the scope, tracked toward the second target in a green-white blur. Within milliseconds, he had acquisition and…

Bang!

Bolan already had the stationary target in view. The guy near the door had jumped up and was obviously panicked, trying to figure out who was shooting at them and from where. Bolan pressed the stock tighter against his shoulder, elevated the sight to compensate for the shift in the last sentry's height.

Bang!

The Executioner was up and moving toward the motel, and had closed the distance by half before the last body hit the ground. He was nearly on top of the motel when the first reactionaries began to appear. Several doors opened at once, and men in various stages of dress—all toting pistols—spilled from the lighted doorways and made themselves perfect and immediate targets.

Bolan pressed with the assault, triggering the FNC in controlled bursts and taking the closest one in the chest. The man's pistol flew from his grasp as his body slammed against the open door. He left a red streak on the door as his body slid to the ground. Bolan took cover behind a narrow post in time to avoid a flurry of shots from another man who had managed to bring his pistol into play. Bolan heard several of the rounds as they moved close past his ears with an angry buzz, or slapped into the post and drove splinters in every direction.

He spun on his heel, going to a crouch, and triggered the FNC from his lower position. The 5.56 .45 mm NATO rounds slammed into the shooter's intestines and continued upward until exiting his back. Gaping holes exploded from the high-velocity rounds that splattered blood and flesh everywhere, the impact slamming the man's body against the brick facade of the motel. Bolan returned to cover behind the post as he yanked one of the grenades from his harness—an M83-HC white smoker—and thumbed away the spoon. He counted off two seconds before rolling the grenade along the sidewalk bordering the motel.

Smoke immediately began to fill the area, and Bolan used

the cover to get in a better position for his offensive. The Executioner reached a door to the motel where one of the dead gunmen lay. He prepared a second grenade, this one an M14 incendiary, and tossed it onto the center of the king-size bed in the middle of the room. The thin bedding would be no match for the twenty-six ounces of TH3 mixture. The bed immediately burst into flames.

Bolan proceeded. A few stray shots bounced near him, but the white smoke was quite effective in masking his movements. The warrior nearly walked into another Mafia crewman. The guy's head exploded under the sudden pressure of close shots, and his mangled corpse spun wildly before falling to the ground accidentally killed by one of his own.

Bolan continued his offensive, catching another hood off guard and shooting him in the stomach. The FNC was a fantastic weapon. While it was a high-velocity assault weapon, it was lightweight and compact enough to use with the same effectiveness as a pistol. The fact it chambered heavy caliber, high-velocity ammunition seemed only a plus in these circumstances.

The Executioner broke through the smoke and saw two guys moving into position on his right, obviously trying to determine if it was possible to come in behind him. It was a poor attempt at a flanking maneuver. Bolan dropped to one knee, raised the FNC to his shoulder and sighted on the pair. He took the first one in the chest with a 3-round burst, the slugs punching through the man's heart and one lung. The second he caught a bit higher, only one of the three rounds landing on target, punching through his chin and shattering his jaw. The force of the bullet ripped away flesh and bone, and tore away most of the lower part of the guy's face and neck. Bolan followed up immediately with a double tap to the stomach.

Something suddenly seized him from behind, jarring the

weapon from its position. Bolan was yanked to his feet, and the tension in both his throat and lower back made it immediately obvious that his attacker was big, muscular and very strong. The Executioner tried to twist away from the headlock, but his opponent's muscle mass quickly canceled that idea. Bolan had managed to hold on to his FNC, so he let his feet come off the ground as he rammed the stock between his legs. The grunt of pain was accompanied by a sudden loosening of the hold.

Bolan twisted inward and drove the stock into his opponent's knee a second time. The blow caused the attacker to let go entirely. The Executioner didn't wait to size up his assailant, instead swinging the weapon upward against the man's chin. The guy was big—*damn big*—but his head snapped backward with the impact, his teeth clacking together audibly. Bolan produced the Desert Eagle in one fluid motion and immediately squeezed the trigger. The slug punched a dime-sized hole through the big mobster's chest and left an exit hole the size of a fist, taking a good chunk of the guy's spine with it. The force lifted him off the ground, and he landed in the doorway from which he'd emerged in a crumpled heap.

There were more shouts of confusion, and men were now running away from the area, no longer interested in sticking around. That was okay with Bolan. They didn't pose a threat as long as they didn't have time to regroup, and since he'd be keeping an eye on their fearless leader, Bolan didn't think that would happen for some time. He continued going through each of the rooms, methodically eliminating any of the opposition who had chosen to stay and fight rather than get the hell out.

Less than five minutes elapsed before Bolan had completed inspecting each room, periodically dumping an incendiary grenade on a bed. The flames were beginning to come through the roof in some areas by the time Bolan headed back toward his vehicle. It wouldn't take long for someone to spot the smoke and call the fire department, but by the time they got there Bolan surmised there wouldn't be much left for them to find.

That was okay. He'd completed his mission here in San Francisco—at least part of it. He'd taken out Pescia's men; next on the list was Lenzini's little electronic operation nestled in the heart of the city. Once he'd dealt with that, Bolan would move on to the next location in Los Angeles, and finally to Seattle. Then he'd go back to Boston or Washington, or wherever Lenzini was holed up, and he'd chop off the head of the operation. By that time, he expected all of the players would be in place, including those in the NIF.

Yeah, it would be their final exit.

8

Washington, D.C.

"I don't mean to seem ungrateful," Tyra MacEwan said. "But is this *really* necessary?"

"Yes, ma'am," replied the guy called Ironman. "It's absolutely necessary."

"I thought the danger was over," she said, pressing.

He shrugged, and while the gesture seemed almost nonchalant, MacEwan could see the concern in the man's hard blue eyes. "We did too, but it would seem there's some new players involved. Now, we've got guys downstairs…good guys. They'll keep an eye on you until we can find out what's going on."

"But I don't *want* to stay here," MacEwan protested. "I want to go back home."

He shook his head. "Look, Tyra, I can understand your frustration, believe me."

She put her hands on her hips and looked at him, raising one eyebrow to signal her skepticism. "Can you?"

"Hell, yeah," he replied with a genuine tone. "If I were you, I wouldn't want to be cooped up in this hole. Still, orders are orders. Listen, some very important people want me and my partners to make sure the air keeps moving in and out of you. When this is cleared up, you can go wherever the hell you want for as long as you want. Okay?"

MacEwan sighed, but knew she didn't have much choice. She knew the big stranger was only doing his job, and it wasn't for kicks. If MacEwan had learned anything about Matt Cooper, it was that he didn't waste his time with idle tasks. She didn't think his friends would be any different in that regard. No, if they really thought there was something to this, then that had to be enough for her.

"My mom will be safe?"

The man nodded and smiled as he headed for the door. "Yeah, we made sure of that. Anybody gets within a hundred feet of her, and they won't know what hit them. In the meantime, I've got to split. Lock and bolt this door behind me."

She nodded and followed him to the door. As she started to close it behind him she said, "Hey, uh—"

"Yeah?"

"Listen, just wanted to say thanks. And when you see Matt and Jack, tell them I said hi."

He winked. "You got it."

Then he was gone, and MacEwan locked herself up tight just as he'd instructed. She looked around at the sparse apartment nestled in the northern downtown area of D.C. Well, she hadn't planned to come back from vacation so damned soon, but that was the breaks. Her mother was safe, and that was the most important thing to her.

MacEwan went over to a desk in one corner of the room where Ironman had told her she'd find everything she needed. It was too bad she didn't know what that meant, since she wasn't even sure what was going on yet. Damn it! So just what was she supposed to do, sit here and twiddle her thumbs? Surf the Internet? She'd thought Cooper's people had pulled everything they needed from her so they could straighten out this mess, and now here she was once again— just as a week ago—locked away in secret hoping to stay alive. Well, this just wasn't—

The ringing phone on the desk startled her from her day-dreaming. She looked at it a moment, letting it ring a couple of times and wondering if she should answer it. Well, it wasn't going to answer itself. She cautiously picked up the receiver.

"Hello?"

"Miss MacEwan?" The tone of the voice that greeted her was gruff and resolute.

She didn't recognize it, and almost immediately she replied, "I'm afraid you have the wrong number, sir. There's—"

"Miss MacEwan, it's okay. I know it's you because *I'm* the one who arranged to put you there. I'm a close friend of Matt Cooper's."

"Well, then that's another story entirely," MacEwan began with a purposeful tone, absently putting her hand on her hip as if the caller could see the disgust. "Do you have *any* idea what you people have put me through? Why aren't Matt or Jack around to—"

"Miss MacEwan, I don't have time to explain all of the details right now," the voice continued, but the tone was gentler. "Now, I know you've been through a lot, but we need your help."

"I think I've helped enough already."

"Yes, yes you have. And I wouldn't dispute that with you for a minute." There was a pause and MacEwan wasn't sure if she should reply or not. "But I'm afraid we've hit a snag, and I think you're one of the few people who can help us."

MacEwan shook her head and sighed deeply. Once again, she was allowing herself to be talked into the middle of something, and she didn't have the first clue what that *something* was. "I guess I should hear you out. Frankly, I owe my life and the life of my family to you people, and especially to Cooper and Jack. I guess if you tell me that this is serious, I'm inclined to believe it."

"It is *very* serious. When you had discussions with our

technical advisors here, you indicated that there was some sort of program, if you will, that allowed us to back the NIF out of our system."

"That's right, and I showed them the programs and algorithms required to do that," she replied. "What's happened?"

"Someone's overridden your work, and they're rapidly undoing everything we've done."

"I'm afraid I still don't understand. The people I talked to were sharp as tacks, especially Bear. They knew as much, if not more, about these kinds of large systems than any particular group I've worked with. Surely they possess the expertise—"

"Expertise isn't the problem," the man replied. "The problem is much larger than that. Listen, I'm going to put you on our speaker system with Bear and our team. I'll let him describe the issue to you."

"Okay." MacEwan began humming some long-forgotten country song, but her wait wasn't long enough to finish the first verse.

"Tyra, this is Bear."

"Well, Bear," MacEwan replied, actually glad to hear the warm, deep voice; it was a voice that possessed such soothing and confident tone. "Listen, I forgot to thank you for helping me out before."

"Don't mention it. But there's a way you could return the favor."

"So I hear. What's the story?"

"We've managed to isolate the network Rhatib created for Nicolas Lenzini, but it would seem that someone else is trying to manipulate the system and get control of Carnivore again. The algorithms look similar to Rhatib's, but—"

"I know what you're going to say," MacEwan interrupted. "He's in custody."

"Exactly," Bear said. "Which tells *us* that somebody else is running the show now, somebody with the technical know-how and the ability to manipulate this network system," he said.

"What does that have to do with me?"

There was a long pause—one that MacEwan sensed was purposeful—and then a chilling sense of foreboding washed over her in that moment. "What's going on? Please...tell me," she said.

"We think it's Dr. Shurish."

"Malcolm?" MacEwan resisted the urge to slam the phone into the cradle. Instead, she said, "Ridiculous! I've known Malcolm Shurish ever since I started with DARPA. He's a brilliant and dedicated scientist, not to mention the fact he's been a good friend and mentor to me. What proof do you have?"

"None yet, but we have it on pretty good authority that he sent someone to follow Cooper."

"Okay, so what?"

"Shurish met him once, at which time someone tried to kill both of them," Kurtzman said.

"Precisely," MacEwan said, "someone *did* try to blow them up. You're suggesting that was Shurish? He rigged this whole thing to make it look like he was an intended target?"

"We don't know for sure that he had anything to do with that," Kurtzman said, "but that's not the issue. The issue is that he sent a Department of Defense investigator to find Cooper. He didn't have any reason to do that. Cooper was a contracted scientist. He wasn't an official employee of DARPA, and he wasn't on any type of watch list. Since he'd never even been inside the system, Shurish had no reason to put a tail on him. Most people would have accepted the explanation from the powers-that-be—an explanation by the way that came directly from the Pentagon—but instead he went out on his own. That doesn't make any sense to us."

"So because he does something crazy you automatically

suspect him of espionage and computer fraud?" MacEwan was struggling to control her anger.

"Tyra, listen to me for a moment," Kurtzman said quietly.

"All right," she said, trying to keep her voice calm. This whole thing was becoming rather ridiculous. How was she supposed to keep her patience in this thing? Less than two weeks had passed since she'd met Cooper, and since that time she'd been kidnapped, bound and gagged, beat up, shot at, and generally moved around the world like a freight package. Now she was being told by Cooper's people—people she'd come to trust—that one of the few friends she thought she had left was possibly working for a known member of organized crime *and* possibly even the New Islamic Front.

"You and I both know that every criminal leaves a signature."

"Like a bomb maker," MacEwan interjected. "Okay, I'm with you so far."

"They know we shut them down. If we try to go back in there, they're going to see us immediately and shut us out. You, on the other hand, they aren't familiar with. Rhatib's the only one who knows your computer fingerprints, and he's locked up as tight as a drum."

"So, you want me to go inside the system and see if I can figure out who else may be buried in Carnivore."

"Actually, we have Carnivore under full surveillance. It's not even that difficult. We want you to get inside Lenzini's networks because that's the source of this trouble. It's a chance to close that end of the hole, and to catch whoever's behind this."

"I don't know," MacEwan said. "You're asking an awful lot. I love my country just as much as the next person, but—"

"Look at it this way. It will give you a chance to prove Shurish is innocent. If he is, he's got nothing to worry about."

MacEwan finally agreed. "All right, I'll do it. Okay?"

"Thank you. Trust me when I say, Tyra, it's all going to work out."

"Oh yeah?" she said. "Then why do I feel so terrible?"

Jonesville, Virginia

THROUGH THE BINOCULARS Abdalrahman scanned the road that led from Lee Penitentiary, then checked his watch.

He sighed with anticipation. Through some type of electronic black magic, Shurish had managed to glean information that a "high-profile" prisoner was being transferred from Lee to a place called Marion, which Shurish advised was in Illinois. The transfer was approved by Homeland Security, which immediately flagged it as extremely sensitive and indicated the prisoner occupied a central role in terrorist activities. Abdalrahman immediately suspected the prisoner was his beloved nephew, and this presented an opportunity to recover his only surviving blood relative before he passed forever beyond their reach.

Abdalrahman was definitely ready for some action; it had been awhile since he'd operated in the field and been able to taste victory against his sworn enemy. The colonel was convinced that it was Sadiq they were transferring, but if he was wrong then they would simply kill the prisoner and cut their losses. Shurish didn't possess the same level of expertise as Sadiq, but he was good enough to complete the work. And when the time came, Abdalrahman would insure Shurish died right along with Nicolas Lenzini and his cronies. Still, while it was a risk to attempt to free his nephew, it was a calculated risk.

Abdalrahman had brought the very best of his small force for this mission. Like him, they were all dressed in camouflage fatigues and equipped with AK-47 assault rifles. They also had half a dozen HE grenades and one disposable rocket launcher, a variant of the U.S.-made M72A2 LAW. They were ready to face a small army, if necessary, and Abdalrahman had no doubts that Sadiq would be under heavy guard.

The former mujiahideen soldier pressed the binoculars to his eyes once more, and a smile formed as he watched light reflect off metal. In the distance, he could see the convoy approaching. According to the intelligence Shurish had gathered, they were transporting the prisoner to a nearby airport. Sending a chopper into the prison was too risky, since it was quite easy to shoot down a helicopter. Stopping a heavily armed escort of vehicles was more risky, particularly since the road to the airfield was only three miles. Not much time to launch an ambush, and the escort was very close to reinforcements.

What this group obviously hadn't counted on was the skill and expertise of Abdalrahman's men, and the resolve of the NIF. Not only was Sadiq important to Abdalrahman personally, he was also the technical genius behind their plans to seize control of American defense systems. They would use those defense systems against the Americans in a way never before imagined. A rescue attempt was worth the risk.

Thus, while the distance between the prison and the airfield was short, there was an imperfection in the defense, a flaw in their thinking that Abdalrahman meant to work fully to his advantage. On the road to the airfield, the convoy would have to cross a small, covered bridge with width and length restrictions that only permitted one vehicle to cross at a time, and in only one direction.

Abdalrahman shifted slightly in the tree, moving his legs some to work the blood through them. He'd been sitting in position for several hours, his disciplined mind refusing to let his body move more than an inch or two in any direction as he watched and waited for the right moment. It was now approaching in the form of the escort convoy. The convoy consisted of a Humvee, a Ford Bronco in the middle—which would contain their prisoner—and a trailing sedan. The road would wind its way through the gentle rolling hillsides of southern Virginia, and eventually they would pass directly under Abdalrahman's vantage point.

Abdalrahman lifted a walkie-talkie to his lips and said, "Units stand by, the targets are approaching."

The first order of business would be to separate the escort units from the transport vehicle, and the explosives rigged to the bridge would deal quite nicely with that. Then they would sweep and clear any resistance, and if Allah was with them— and Abdalrahman believed this to be true—then Sadiq would be there and he would be safe.

The Humvee rolled into view over a rise and Abdalrahman was careful not to move. Undoubtedly, the enemy wasn't stupid, and the escorts would be watching the roads and the overhead areas. They knew the bridge was vulnerable, as much as the NIF assault team did, but in their minds there was probably little risk since nobody was even supposed to know about the transfer.

The convoy slowed considerably as the lead vehicle passed under Abdalrahman's position. The transport vehicle stopped just shy of the bridge entrance, as he'd planned. The sedan would probably do the same, but his men would take care of that. The Humvee contained the heaviest opposition, so it was the most natural target for what followed.

There was a moment that seemed frozen in time as the first charges being detonated resounded through the valleylike surroundings. As the repetitive booming noises fell silent, there was a creaking sound, followed by crackling noises, and suddenly the covered bridge dropped away and into the thirty-foot ravine it had spanned only moments before.

Abdalrahman took his cue and dropped from the tree, landing hard on the hood of the Bronco where the metal caved under his feet. The colonel maintained his balance, and then waited for a response from the interior. The sedan screeched to a halt and several men jumped from the vehicle, drawing their guns, but since they were focused on Abdalrahman and the carnage ahead of them, they weren't prepared for an attack on their rear flank.

Abdalrahman didn't flinch as his men jumped from the trees and began to fire on the sedan's occupants. One man fell immediately under the onslaught of bullets, the force of the rounds slamming him into the door window he'd intended to use as cover and shattering the glass. He slid to the ground and pools of blood immediately began to form in the dust.

One of the others in the sedan turned and managed to get a shot off before the high-velocity rounds split his chest and skull wide open. The man's body crumpled, his tender flesh no match for that kind of destructive force. The remaining two guards were dispatched in much the same way, and even as the escorting guards poured from the Bronco to render assistance, a grenade tossed into the sedan by one of the NIF soldiers eliminated any chance of survivors.

Abdalrahman immediately opened up on the guards as they tried to evacuate the Bronco and seek cover. He shot two clean through the head, and a third managed to get about four steps before being caught in a cross fire by Abdalrahman and several of his men. Abdalrahman jumped from the roof of the Bronco and landed next to the rear door. He nodded to his men, who stepped forward and yanked the door open.

A man in uniform jumped from the seat, an M-16 A-2 automatic rifle in his hands, and began to fire on Abdalrahman's team. Two of his men fell under the vicious counterattack before they were able to bring the enemy down with a hail of gunfire from the AK-47s. Dust settled and an eerie quiet ensued following the eradication of the last of the resistance.

Abdalrahman stepped forward cautiously and looked into

the darkened interior. There sat Sadiq Rhatib, tears streaming down his cheeks. He didn't look any worse for the wear, and—although Abdalrahman suspected he'd had quite an ordeal—it did not appear he had been beaten or starved in any way. Abdalrahman signaled for his men's assistance and they gently removed Rhatib from the Bronco and detached him from the chains using the dead guard's keys.

Abdalrahman then stepped forward and held his nephew's face before planting a kiss on either shoulder.

"I am thankful you are still alive," he told Rhatib.

"I am thankful that you found me when you did, Uncle," Rhatib replied. "When I heard I was being moved, I was certain you would never be able to find me."

"I almost did not," Abdalrahman replied. He decided not to mention that it was actually Shurish they had to thank. He didn't want to make it harder for Rhatib when the time came for them to eliminate Shurish. "I am glad you are now safe. This will never happen again, Sadiq. I promise you that."

"And I believe you." He looked around and added, "I am sure they will send reinforcements quickly once it is discovered they did not arrive at the airfield."

"Yes, come," his uncle replied. "You have very important work to finish. Within a few days, we will bring America to its knees."

9

San Francisco, California

Mack Bolan managed to intercept Gino Pescia in an alley on the back side of his club, just as the rogue gangster was climbing into his car.

Bolan stepped from the shadows, Beretta 93-R in hand, and said, "Hi, Gino."

"Ah!" Pescia jumped and shook his fist at Bolan. "Damn it, Frankie, you scared the shit outta me!"

"Really," Bolan deadpanned. "Why are you so nervous? Your color is terrible. You look as if you've seen a ghost. Now, is that because you know Lenzini's going to put a price on your head so large that every contract hitter around will be flocking to San Francisco in the next forty-eight hours? Oh, no, it couldn't be that. Maybe it's because you were supposed to meet me and you didn't, because you sent your goons to kill me instead."

"Look, Frankie, I had nothing to do with that," Pescia said, raising his hands. "I didn't order the hit on you."

"But you know who did?"

The mobster nodded.

Bolan aimed the pistol and said, "Get in the car. We're taking a ride."

"To where?"

"I'll tell you once we're moving," Bolan said. He waved the pistol slightly as a reminder and then climbed into the passenger side of the sports car while Pescia got behind the wheel.

The Executioner knew he'd have to watch this guy. Pescia was slippery for sure, but Bolan had to believe he wasn't the one who'd ordered the hit. The guy didn't have that kind of clout, and it didn't make sense for Pescia to have Bolan eliminated when he'd just cut the guy a break. No, somebody else had pushed the button on that one, and Bolan planned to find out who it was.

"So where are we going?" Pescia asked once they were away from the club and moving.

"City of Angels," Bolan replied casually.

Pescia looked at him. "I'm not packed yet."

"You can buy some new stuff when you get there."

"I got a club to run, Frankie," he pressed. "I can't just—"

"You want to stay alive?" Bolan asked him, fixing Pescia with a harsh gaze. "Then you'll do as I say. Otherwise, you can take your chances with Lenzini. Now, who ordered the hit on me?"

"Well, I can't be sure about this now, but as I understand—"

"Don't be mealymouthed, Gino," Bolan said interrupting. "I don't have time for it."

Pescia's expression turned meek. "Sorry. Listen, word has it that Serge ordered the job."

"That doesn't make sense. Why would Grano send me out here and then order me whacked?"

"I guess he figured once you found me, you didn't really matter anymore."

"I'm not buying that. Where did you get the information?"

"Hey, look, I don't care if you are toting a piece, there's no way I'm telling you who my sources are. Okay?" Pescia was animated now, throwing up his hands and talking rapidly. "You don't think I'd ask you who whispers in your ears at night, so why would you do me that way? We're supposed to be on the same team, Frankie."

"Yeah, all right," Bolan said and he made a show of holstering his Beretta. "It's obvious some broad told you, so I shouldn't be nosy. Fair enough."

Pescia was silent for a time, and Bolan let him stew. He could tell, looking at the guy's profile, the shadows occasionally lit by streetlights or oncoming cars, that the guy was giving serious thought to his present situation. He was either looking for a way out, or he was concerned about the upcoming skirmish with the NIF. In either case, Bolan sensed there was still something the guy wasn't telling him, but he figured there was another time to worry about it. This was the moment to dangle the bait.

"You know where Lenzini's operation for the Arabs is in L.A., right?" he asked.

"Yeah."

"And you also said your guys are ready for this fight?"

"I don't really have anybody up in Los Angeles," Pescia admitted. "Most of the crew I have is down here, hiding."

"Well, let's go round them up," Bolan replied.

Bolan wanted Pescia to see firsthand what had happened to his crew. That would give him the leverage he needed to bring the small-time hood around, and better control any conflict against Lenzini's people and the NIF. He could work the angles on this end, and now that Stony Man intended to solicit Tyra MacEwan's involvement, so much the better. At least he wouldn't have to worry about what was happening on the other side of the country—Brognola could handle that in his sleep.

Pescia drove them straight to the motel on the edge of town, but he wasn't prepared for what he found. The place shrouded in smoke, some areas still in flames, while other parts consisted of little more than charred wood and smoldering ruins. Bolan could see Pescia was surprised by the carnage, and he meant to play that hand as long as he could.

"Don't stop," Bolan ordered him as they hugged the shoulder to get around the emergency vehicles.

"Wh-what the fuck happened, man?" Pescia stammered.

"I don't know," Bolan said, "but I bet I can guess. Who else knew about this place besides you and me?"

"Just some of my guys," Pescia replied. "You know, the boys at the club. And I've got a contact up in Seattle."

"Nobody on Lenzini's end?"

"Nope."

"You sure?" Bolan pressed. "You sure you didn't tell anybody there on the East Coast? Not even maybe Grano or Ape?"

"No, no," Pescia said. "I swear, I haven't told anyone. Maybe a handful of people knew."

"Well, obviously, that was one too many," Bolan said, jerking his thumb at the destruction as they drove past. "Either that, or the NIF did this."

"But how?"

"Somebody screwed you," Bolan replied, seeing his opportunity to nail the coffin shut. "Somebody who knew about this and is loyal to the NIF ratted you out. Isn't it obvious, Gino? They saw you as a threat and they figured there was only one way to eliminate that threat. They did a number on you."

"Yeah, well, who is 'they,' Frankie?" Pescia asked. "Eh? Can you tell me that? How do I know *you* aren't working for the Arabs and arranged all of this?"

"Because Lenzini's still working with them, and if I was all for his plan to pal around with the rag heads I would have capped you by now," Bolan said sharply. "But you look pretty alive to me, Gino, so I'd cut the smart-ass bit."

"Yeah, okay," Pescia grumbled. "You're right. I guess I do have somebody friendly to the Arabs in my backyard. I need to find out whoever it is and take care of business."

"Wrong," Bolan said quickly. "What you need to do is start listening to me. You can't go back to your club and slap nobody around, Gino. If somebody there arranged this, then they know you're bound to find out about the hit here, and come around looking for some payback. Instead of winding up avenging it, you'll just wind up dead."

"I can't let this go, Frankie," Pescia said.

"Nobody says you have to. Look, for now the most important thing is to get another crew together. Safest place to do that is in L.A. Lenzini won't be looking for you to go there, and neither will the Arabs. We can get our shit together. I may even know a few guys I can call up who would love a piece of this."

"Yeah, yeah...you're right." Pescia slapped the steering wheel and grinned. "You're abso-fucking-lutely right, Frankie. Let's get out of here!"

"Now you're talking," Bolan said.

Los Angeles, California

IT TOOK the Executioner and Pescia five hours to reach L.A., and the mobster immediately drove them to an apartment a few blocks from Santa Monica Beach, which provided a great view of the ocean. The place was small but nice—affordable in a middle-class kind of way—and Bolan could immediately tell this guy had done well with the drug-set in that particular neighborhood. The difference between pushing on the streets and pushing toward the kind of clientele Pescia dealt with was a matter of numbers. A dope-head on ninety-eight was going to pay maybe twenty-five or thirty for a piece of rock, while someone down at the Marina, planning the next party on their yacht, would go four times that price for the equivalent amount of powder. Of course, the rock might be laced with rat poison or laundry detergent versus the powder containing talcum, but that's where the differences ended.

It was a strange economy when it came to drug dealing, and only those who knew how to talk the talk *and* walk the walk stood any chance of staying in business on the Gold Coast. In either case, Pescia had quite a little enterprise going for himself, and Bolan figured it wouldn't take much to bring the small drug emperor to his knees when the opportunity presented itself.

"So, what's your plan?" Pescia said, throwing aside the curtains to let in the dawn light. He went to the bar and made himself a drink. He offered one to Bolan, but the soldier declined with a shake of his head.

"You tell me," Bolan said. "This is your territory. How many guys do you think you can get?"

Pescia shrugged as he dropped ice cubes into his glass. "I don't know, maybe ten, fifteen at best."

"That's not a lot, Gino."

"Frankie, what do you want me to say, huh?" Pescia said in protest, throwing the tongs on the bar and reaching for a decanter full of what looked like bourbon. "Everybody I had lined up is probably dead. If not, they're most certainly in hiding and not going to be coming out to play for some time. What, you think I can snap my fingers and guys just line up around here? It took a lot of doing to get the guys I had."

"All right, settle down," Bolan said. "I just asked a question."

"Yeah, well, I just gave you an answer."

"Okay, so you can get ten guys. Tell you what, you provide the manpower, I'll provide the firepower."

"Just how do you plan to do that?"

"That's my business," Bolan said.

"Okay, so we get some guys together and you get them some guns. So what? We just going to sit on our asses and do nothing? Maybe wait for the Arabs to stick it to us again? We're sitting ducks as long as we're not doing something."

"Right," Bolan said. "And that's where my plan comes in.

Look, the whole reason you're in hot water with Lenzini right now is because you won't play ball with the Arabs."

Pescia snorted. "Does that surprise you? You knocked the shit out of me and burned their little club in D.C. to the ground. You didn't actually expect me to go back to him with that message, did you? You know who blamed me for that? Serge and the boys. They said I didn't have any balls to let some punk walk over me like that. And then they said that the Arabs were going to blame *us* for what happened, and I was going to be the scapegoat if anything nasty came down."

"You mean they were going to burn you to save their own asses?" Bolan asked, acting completely surprised by Pescia's woefully told tale.

"Yeah! Can you believe that shit? I give them the best years of my life, and come out here regularly and bring in my contacts. I've made Lenzini quite a bit of cash here. And that's how I get thanked! They threaten to turn me over to the Arabs."

"That doesn't sound like they're protecting the brotherhood," Bolan said in his most sympathetic tone. He shook his head and clucked his tongue. "That's not what the Family used to be about. The rules have changed."

"You're damn straight they've changed!" Pescia said, downing the last of his drink and pouring himself another. This time, he didn't add any ice.

Bolan had to keep the guy talking. The drunker he got the more vulnerable he was likely to be, and Bolan could pump him for valuable information. Intelligence was always the key in bringing down the enemy, and with guys like Pescia it was child's play to get that information. Most people had a weakness, whether it was alcohol, drugs, sex, or money, and Bolan had learned how to work those weaknesses to his advantage.

"There's no more camaraderie, you know what I mean?" Pescia asked, taking another hard swallow from the glass as his face started to turn red. "There's just a lot of talk, and making deals with guys who would just as soon slit your throat or sleep with your wife than do real business. That's what I do, you know, Frank? I do *real* business. I don't screw nobody, and I don't shoot off my mouth to nobody."

Except to me, Bolan thought.

Pescia finished his drink and poured another, then dropped stiffly into a nearby chair. "I just want to get these guys back, man. I want these guys to pay for what they did to me."

"I know, Gino," Bolan said. "And I can help you do that."

"You can?"

Bolan noticed as he sat down on a chair directly across from Pescia that the mobster's eyes were starting to look glazed. He was tired and strongly affected by the alcohol since they hadn't eaten anything on the trip. This was the most critical point for Bolan, and he had to make his move before time simply ran out. He had to put all of the pieces in place, and be ready for the NIF when it made its move. If he could manipulate Pescia, push the guy just a little bit further and earn his full trust, he'd be able to pull it off. Neither Lenzini nor the NIF would even know what hit them until it was much too late.

"I can," Bolan continued. "I can help you take back your business. You're just going to have to trust me, man. You do trust me, don't you?"

Pescia nodded blankly, his speech slurring as he replied, "Yeah, Frankie. Yeah, I trust you."

"Good. Now why don't you tell me where you've set up this base for the Arab's network?"

Predictably, Pescia began to spill his guts.

Washington, D.C.

ONCE SADIQ RHATIB HAD rested, changed clothes and consumed a hearty meal, he went to work on the network systems. There were still remnants of Carnivore in their control—sleepers he'd left in the programming algorithms—and all he had to do was activate them. But there would be a right time and place for that. As long as the programs weren't active, they were virtually undetectable. Besides, it was going to be some time before word got to the right people that he'd escaped, and by that time he'd have the system in place.

The first order of business would be to start bringing Nicolas Lenzini's network programs online. Rhatib's uncle had already gone to meet the American criminal at his estate in Arlington, and once he'd gotten the signal, his uncle would terminate their relationship with Lenzini—permanently.

Rhatib could remember arguing with his uncle about bringing Lenzini on in the first place. He didn't trust the American crime syndicate, and he *certainly* didn't trust Lenzini and his people. First, they had allowed the Garden of Allah to be destroyed, and risked little to protect such an important investment. That club, while seemingly only a physical structure, had served a multitude of purposes including providing a safehouse for soldiers in the NIF who had conducted operations within American borders. It had even served as a temporary sanctuary for Rhatib during the few months he'd spent here in America, working to perfect the system they would eventually use to control U.S. defensive systems.

Still, he did have to admit that Lenzini had come through on providing the network coverage necessary to implement their plan. They now had to bring certain systems online in a certain sequence, so as not to arouse the suspicions of those government agencies that were electronically monitoring for specific kinds of traffic. The nice thing was that they wouldn't be looking for Rhatib in this exercise, since they had no way to tie Lenzini with the NIF.

"Auxiliary systems are online and waiting," Malcolm

Shurish announced with a triumphant beating of his fist on a nearby table.

Rhatib only nodded, trying to remain focused on the tasks at hand. They were working from Shurish's hideaway retreat, a small Georgian-style house nestled away in the Appalachian foothills he'd purchased some time back. Shurish had the perfect excuse to work from home, since he'd rigged the bomb in his office, and repair and remodeling efforts were still underway. Shurish had remarked about how long it took the government to complete anything, but somehow Rhatib and Abdalrahman hadn't really caught onto the joke.

"What's the next step?" Shurish asked.

"We must insure that each system can talk to the others," Rhatib said. "Even though the networks are up and running, it will take at least twenty-four hours to run all of the necessary diagnostics."

"We may not have twenty-four hours," Shurish replied. "Your uncle wants us ready to go as soon as possible."

"My uncle trusts *me* to decide that, Doctor," Rhatib said, his face reddening. "I am the expert here."

"On some of it maybe," Shurish replied. The scientist was older and more experienced, and he was not about to concede to some boy wonder just off the boat.

"What is that supposed to mean?"

"It means that we are supposed to work together," Shurish said. He walked around the table until he could look Rhatib straight in the eye. "It means that we both want the same thing."

"And that is?"

"The victory of the New Islamic Front," Shurish declared.

"But I would guess," Rhatib replied, "that you would also like to see your system up and running?"

"Why not?" Shurish asked. "I don't deny it for a moment. It is a work of art, and a demonstration of man's genius in the world of technology. We can now communicate at light-ning-fast speeds with very little effort and with devices no wider than the nail of my smallest finger. Nothing in the U.S. government's present arsenal can even come close to that. With this system, we will be able to predict the response of missile defense systems three-times faster than those systems can actually respond. We can intercept and scramble commu-nications and disperse communication packets across multi-ple locations so that it can never be traced or pulled back together. And, most importantly, we will be able to garble radio, microwave, satellite and broadband communication frequencies so that not only will American forces not be able to talk with allied systems, but they will not even be able to talk among themselves. This is the SuperNet we are about to implement. It is a power unequaled in human history, and one which we are about to unleash upon the entire world. It is my life's work. Why wouldn't I want to see it come to life?"

Rhatib watched Shurish with fascination, and in that mo-ment he realized the man was insane. He'd come to believe in his own infallibility, and put all of his faith in this techno-logical wonder. There was no longer any strong sense of re-ligious conviction to be found in him. He no longer believed in Allah, and it was doubtful he even believed in the NIF's cause. It was apparent the only thing Shurish had come to be-lieve in was himself.

And that made him as dangerous as their enemies.

10

Tyra MacEwan concluded her study of the SuperNet maps and network topologies, leaned back in her chair and shook her head with amazement. She stopped only for a moment to study her surroundings. She felt lonely and nervous, jumping at every sound as if it were the bogie man coming to get her. She chided herself for letting the sounds of the night rattle her cage. She was an adult possessing talent, brains and a .38-caiber snub nose—and she knew how to use all of them.

MacEwan turned back to the subject at hand, studying the network one more time before beginning the real work. Hacking into the internal systems of Lenzini's former dot-com companies wasn't very hard to do. It didn't look like the guy had a clue about network security. Bear had managed to get inside the system within a few minutes, and had sent the crack codes onto her. Now it was just a matter of looking for the unseen, and drawing the unusual out of what appeared, on the surface, to be quite ordinary.

Simple software firewalls protecting a basic Transmission Control Protocol/Internet Protocol configuration over a worldwide network was the first oddity MacEwan noticed. On the surface, the information these systems collected and stored seemed routine, such as customer online orders and the like. However, upon a more detailed scrutiny, Bear's people had discovered that something was amiss. First, the information stored inside the network wasn't even valid. Bogus names, addresses, credit card numbers; the list went on and on. Additionally, there was no consistency in any of the internal data or the relational records. No such products existed, and there was absolutely no real-time transaction information stored anywhere. There were no real purchases, deposits, credits or debits, or any real accounts holding real money. The account numbers held internally on the systems weren't even consistent.

MacEwan knew immediately what the architects were attempting to do. It started with the fact they were using basic Internet protocols, and something more along the lines of the hardware technology in place at each of the remote sites. Supposedly, these sites were using mainframes, application and Web servers, and a host of other expensive equipment and cabling, and yet the servers were only running basic TCP/IP communications at slow transmission speeds when they were capable of transmitting information at unparalleled rates.

The TCP/IP communications language actually worked at two different layers. At the higher layer was the Transmission Control Protocol, a program that disassembled messages into smaller and more compact units that were reassembled by another TCP layer on the receiving side. The Internet Protocol, the lower layer of the communications program, actually addressed part of the total message to the same destination, but usually sent each packet disassembled by the TCP layer through different routes.

Rhatib had tried a similar trick after cracking into the Carnivore system, although he'd mixed and matched a variety of programs and scripting languages to do it. Only because MacEwan and Mitch Fowler had worked to create tighter security inside the Carnivore system had she been able to detect Rhatib's handiwork. Finding out what was really going on behind the scenes inside Lenzini's network was another matter entirely.

No, it wasn't going to be easy.

MacEwan needed to know if Malcolm Shurish was really involved in all of this, as Cooper's people suspected. It was possible Shurish was doing something shady, but that didn't make him a bad guy and it *certainly* didn't mean he was a terrorist. After all, Bear or the other man she'd spoken with didn't offer any hard proof that Shurish had anything to do with the New Islamic Front. Shurish had hired MacEwan for her position at DARPA—the government had hired her on his recommendation. She'd come to trust him, and she'd never seen anything to make her believe he was a traitor. And why go to the trouble of trying to make it look like somebody was trying to kill him? Not to mention the fact that he'd killed his secretary in the process of that bombing, and he didn't even know Cooper was anything more than a temporary replacement for MacEwan in her absence.

It just seemed like there had to be another explanation, and MacEwan knew that it was important she find out what was happening inside of Lenzini's network. Bear was at least right about one thing: it would help her prove Shurish was innocent. And if he wasn't, well, then, she would deal with that when the time came—even if she had to do it herself.

MacEwan knew the first step to finding out the real purpose of Lenzini's networked systems was to get past all of the false data he had stored. Obviously, the technical advisors Lenzini had working for him thought they had enough of a facade to maintain the appearance of a legitimate business across the World Wide Web and they had not accounted for the fact that someone with more brains than they had would actually go beyond a cursory inspection. They hadn't been counting on someone like Tyra MacEwan to be poking through their systems.

MacEwan first identified all of the databases Bear's team had confirmed contained erroneous data and began writing an algorithm that would sort the data into hash tables and put them in a temporary location. She also figured she'd have to write a security program to hide her tracks and lock out anyone attempting to access that portion of the communications portal when she was in it. That would make it look as if there was some bug in the system, and by the time they had anyone actually look at the thing, she'd be off and onto the next area.

The other thing MacEwan was counting on was the fact that Cooper was going to take care of the physical sites where the hardware was located. While that end of the system would be down, MacEwan could still work the mystery from her end by pulling the information to her and storing it locally. Bear's team had provided her with quite a sweet setup, actually, with more than enough material on her end to run her own Internet-based business had she really wanted.

Beneath the large desk were two servers. One would run secondary tasks and applications in the background—her codebreakers, hashers and parsers—while the second would act as a server for local databases and information storage retrieval. She would use the laptop system connected to these to run actual programs, and there was also a desktop unit with three broadband connections. One of those connections was designed for Internet access only, one was hooked into the special virtual private government network and support systems that Bear had set up for her, and the last was a backup system that would fire up in the event she lost either of the first two connections. The entire setup was hooked into a freestanding power supply, so a power loss would not affect her in any way.

It took MacEwan almost six hours to complete the first program, but she knew it was going to be a tedious process, and she'd told Bear as much. Nonetheless, it appeared the program was working as it began to sort through the data, organize it, and store into the temporary tables she'd created. Now and again, MacEwan had to shut the program down and make a correction, but she'd dealt with it quickly and in minutes it would be up again and continued working through the massive data on Lenzini's network.

Another two hours passed before a very disturbing pattern began to appear. As the data was pushed aside, MacEwan could see that there was nothing behind it. That wasn't possible though, because all of that data was just stored as relational records in plain, ASCII-based flat files. There wasn't anything more to it. MacEwan was positive she'd find something else behind it, but no such luck. She ran the program for another hour—peeling the data out of the system layer by layer—but after all of that time, there was nothing there. Instead of finding the true information behind the jigsaw puzzle of data, she instead discovered that nothing resided in any of Lenzini's core systems.

MacEwan picked up the telephone and Kurtzman answered on the second ring.

"Are you seeing this?" she asked him.

"No," he replied. "Actually, I'm seeing nothing. And it's what I'm *not* seeing that has me worried."

"Agreed," MacEwan said. "I thought for sure we'd find what we were looking for behind all of that data."

"As did I, but now I'm wondering if maybe that's what whoever designed this system was hoping we'd think. They figured we'd waste our time hashing and parsing through the data."

"And we took the bait."

"Right," Kurtzman said. "I guess our enemy isn't as stupid as we thought. Let me ask you this, just based on what you've seen to this point. Is it possible Shurish had something to do with this?"

"No, I—" MacEwan began, but then she stopped herself. "Wait a minute! It *is* possible, Bear. A few years ago, when I first started working with DARPA, Malcolm was trying to sell some group at the Pentagon on a project he called Operation Poltergeist."

Bear stopped her, and she could hear the rapid clack of keys as he typed something into his system. A moment later, he sighed deeply. "There's nothing in our databanks about it, and there's something to be said for that."

"I don't think he ever published any of his findings. In fact, I don't think he even worked on it through any of DARPA's equipment or systems. He was always very secretive about his work."

"What do you know about this Poltergeist?"

"The entire premise was based on the idea of sorting data in such a way that to the observer it would appear normal. Further investigation of that data, or storing it temporarily in tables, wouldn't reveal anything unusual and at that point most hackers would probably give up. The trick was in the data itself. It was encrypted so that elements of the data were valid, but they weren't in a valid order and each record relation was actually indexed by a secret code."

"I think I'm beginning to understand here," Kurtzman said, "and I'm not sure I like the thought. You're saying that all of the data we just copied out of the system is valid, but it's scrambled."

"Correct. If you think about it, it's actually a brilliant concept."

"Yeah, and it's Shurish's brilliance that scares me."

"We should be more concerned about what this could mean," MacEwan said.

"That is?"

"The coding algorithms used to index the information so they can be resorted and reorganized into something meaningful are actually controlled by an entry code, much in the same fashion Rhatib used to get inside Carnivore. That means we have to find a way to counteract that entry code by sorting through the data and finding out what it really means. We can then write a program that will counteract it…an exit code of a sort."

"I hear a 'but' coming," Kurtzman said.

"Well, I'm sorry to say this but you hear right. The only way to implement this thing is to port it into the systems in assembly language."

"Which means it has to be run locally at each network site," Kurtzman said.

"Either that, or at the source system from where the entry code is actually executed."

"Which would require us to know where, when, and how the NIF plans to use it."

"Precisely."

"Great," Kurtzman finally said after a long pause. "It keeps getting better all the time. I don't suppose there's another alternative?"

"None of which I'm aware," MacEwan replied. "But if you have any suggestions, I'm all ears."

There was only silence.

"While we're bringing up more problems, I think you should also know that I don't possess any real expertise in writing assembly language. I'll need some help."

"Our people have plenty of experience in that," Kurtzman replied. "We'll start working those angles on this end. In the meantime, I assume you'll start trying to crack this code."

"Yes."

"Okay. Let me know if you need anything. And Tyra, we just want you to know that we appreciate everything you've done for us. We know that you've sacrificed a lot."

"As I've told you already, Jack and Cooper saved my neck and I don't know if I'll ever be able to repay that debt. But you just make sure your people keep their end of the bargain and protect my mom."

"You don't have any reason to worry about that," Kurtzman said. "She's in the hands of three of the most able-bodied guys I know."

Boston, Massachusetts

SERGE GRANO SAT in the same chair he'd occupied a hundred times before and tapped his fingers nervously on his knee. He thought about the fact that old man Lenzini had probably kept him waiting on purpose. Nonetheless, Grano couldn't say he really minded. He respected Mr. Lenzini. The same couldn't be said for most of the men. He would have done anything for his boss. He considered the old man brilliant, and he was totally devoted to their cause. Still, he hadn't been comfortable with the idea of working for the Arabs. No, check that—they were working *with* the Arabs. In either case, it didn't make much sense to Grano. They could have just as easily made their money the old-fashioned way.

Grano had to admit that he was probably a dinosaur when it came to business sense for the Family. He was used to the old-fashioned way of doing things: squeezing local business owners for protection, laundering funds in Vegas, and moving everything from one place to another where the highest bidders were waiting. Grano had damn near done it all. In fact, he'd originally started with old man Lenzini when the guy was just small potatoes. His primary job was mule, escorting jewels, chicks, or guns from here to there without drawing attention and without getting screwed by the other side. Yeah, he'd moved just about everything—except dope.

Fortunately, Lenzini had been smart enough not to get into that game, and that's what frosted his ass the most about guys like Pescia. All right, so they wanted to have their own territories and flex their muscles like they were big men. Grano didn't have an issue with that. Except when it started to compromise the old man, or when it drew attention from the Feds. That's where Grano had to draw the line, and it looked like that time had come for Pescia.

Grano looked up at the sound of the door in the wall sliding aside and stood out of respect as Lenzini came in. The troop boss didn't hesitate, though, when Lenzini waved him into his seat. He could tell there was a bit of disgust in Lenzini's tone, but the old man was holding back his temper. His health couldn't afford the kind of venom with which Lenzini had once run his organization. Any overexertion, mental or physical, could be an immediate death sentence.

"Relax, Serge," Lenzini said as he stopped behind his desk. "You're among family. There's no reason to be so god-damned formal."

"Of course, Don Lenzini."

Lenzini said, "I understand the situation in San Francisco turned serious."

"Yes, Don Lenzini."

"You want to explain it to me?"

Grano could only shrug. "We missed hitting Pescia, boss. Our guys jumped too soon, and Lambretta left them in the cold."

"What do you mean?"

"I guess the freaking guy was armed to the teeth," Grano replied.

"Of course he was!" Lenzini spit. "What the fuck did you think would happen, Serge? This guy has one hell of a reputation! He's as loyal as they come, and I planned to use that to our advantage, but because your people jumped too soon, he's going to figure out it was us who sent them! And what do you think he's going to do then, eh?"

"I was talking to him when the hit went down. He'd never suspect it was me that set it up. There's nothing to tie them to us."

"There doesn't have to be," Lenzini replied, settling down after his outburst produced a fit of coughing. "That's my whole point. Nobody else knew he was in town."

"Except Pescia," Grano interjected.

"What do you mean?"

"Something about this Lambretta isn't as loyal as you might think, Don Lenzini." Grano knew he had the old man now. He loved Lenzini, but the guy was brutal and Grano had sworn long ago he'd make sure he never looked bad in front of him. There always had to be someone else to blame. "Yeah, you heard me right. Lambretta went to see Pescia at his club. They apparently had a nice long talk."

"About what?"

"About how he ran because of a Fed at the Garden of Allah."

"You think Gino flipped him?"

Grano shook his head. "Flipped him with what? I don't think Gino could come up with the kind of smack necessary to buy off Lambretta. Besides, the guy is supposed to be loyal. I think he was probably just looking to take over the operation once you gave the order to have Gino whacked, and this gave him a chance to scope the territory."

"I warned him about screwing us around," Lenzini said, coughing again.

"Well, it would seem that he didn't listen to you very good."

"What do you think we should do about that?"

"I think we better 'find him.'"

"What do you mean 'find him'?" Lenzini asked. "I thought he was still in San Francisco?"

"His tail was one of the team that got whacked. We don't know what happened after that. We know that his hotel room got blown apart, and what we're hearing from our guys inside the cops there is that machine guns were used. We're also hearing that something went down at some motel just outside of town with machine guns and grenades, and they're thinking the two jobs are related."

"So that's what they think, Serge," Lenzini said. "What do *you* think?"

"I was thinking it sounded an awful lot like what went down at the club in D.C."

"That's a good thought." Lenzini was quiet for a long moment, and said, "That's a good thought indeed. I think you could be onto something. I want you to take Ape and go to San Francisco and find Lambretta. And I want Gino brought back here alive like we originally planned."

"Understood, but we have another problem you need to know about. They screwed up in Texas and lost the government broad."

For a moment, Grano thought Lenzini's head would explode off his shoulders. The man's face turned a deep scarlet, and Grano could tell he wanted to unload but that he was holding back. They couldn't afford to lose Lenzini at such a crucial time, and nobody knew that better than Lenzini.

"I can't ask Trabucco to do one simple thing without him fucking it up. And he's got DeLama's kid with him. You know, I'm like an uncle to that kid. You know this, right?"

"I know, Don Lenzini," Grano said softly.

"Well, you're in charge of security and the bulls, Serge, so I expect you'll know how to handle this. Don't bring this petty shit to me. This one time, I'll tell you what you do. You have those guys meet you out on the West Coast. They can help you look for Gino and Lambretta."

"What about Lambretta? You want we should bring him back too?"

"No, I wouldn't waste your time with that."

"So what do you want done with him?"

"I don't care," Lenzini said. "Just see that he doesn't come back."

11

Los Angeles, California

Mack Bolan looked over Pescia's assembled crew, cautious to maintain his air of authority.

He couldn't afford to let the crowd of mobsters think he was soft, but he also had to convince them Gino Pescia was still ultimately in charge of things. That was really the only way he could insure that his plans would succeed while still keeping the loyalty of these men. Bolan searched his near-photographic memory, and after a few minutes he realized that Pescia was rather well-connected on the West Coast. There weren't just soldiers and bulls gathered, but also a few midrankers and even one high-level capo.

What Bolan found most ironic was that he was about to send some of these guys into a situation where they were going to encounter members of the New Islamic Front—if everything went off as planned—and by drawing them out he would be able to destroy both enemy groups. It was risky, but it was all he had to go on, and the Executioner had to play the hand the way it was dealt to him.

"All right, listen up," Pescia said, putting an end to the idle chitchat. "I wanna thank all of you for coming on such short notice. This here is Frankie Lambretta. Some of you might have heard of him."

Bolan quickly scanned their faces, but there were no real acknowledgments of recognition at either his face or his name. That was okay, just as long as they all got a good look. Bolan was planning on a few escaping the upcoming encounter so they could get word back to Grano and the rest—when the time was right.

"Now, Frankie was sent by Don Lenzini to ice me, but when I explained what we were trying to do out here, that plan suddenly changed." Pescia made a funny gesture with his hands, and everyone laughed boisterously. After they'd settled down, Pescia continued, "But we've got a common enemy, guys. The Arabs have taken over, and Don Lenzini's in for a fall unless we do something now."

"How do we know it's the Arabs?" one guy asked.

"Because we saw a bunch of our dead crew in San Francisco," Bolan said. "Somebody blew them all to hell, and we *know* that the only others who knew their location would have been the Arabs. Plus, I talked with Serge Grano back in Boston. He told me that they did something similar in D.C. not that long ago."

"So what's with this powwow?" another asked.

"We're going to get some payback," Bolan replied. "Gino here helped Don Lenzini's people set up the technical site downtown that the rags are going to use for taking over the world, or whatever the hell it is they're planning. We think that once they're up and running, they'll no longer have a use for us and we'll be throwaway."

"There's no way they outnumber us," one of the guys popped off.

"What's your name?" Bolan asked him.

"Ray Donatto," he replied.

"Of the San Fernando Valley Donattos," Pescia added.

The guy nodded respectfully at Pescia.

Yeah, Mack Bolan knew *exactly* who Ray Donatto was, although he hadn't seen any pictures of him since Donatto was a just a snot-nosed hood up and coming in the world. All of the intelligence channels through Brognola's Justice connections had it that Ray Donatto was as nasty and ruthless as they came. Donatto was actually a capo in charge of many of the soldiers working for his father, and had managed to establish quite an empire of his own. Rumors had it he had once taken a chain saw to a Cuban dealer in a drug buy gone sour, and then mailed the remains back to the dealer's spouse. Once word got around he never had any trouble after that, and the repeated attempts by state and federal officials to put him behind bars had failed.

"I've heard of you, Donatto," Bolan said. "No disrespect, but I'd have to disagree with you."

"About what?"

"The mere fact we outnumber the Arabs won't be enough to put them down. We also need to show our muscle, and a hell of a lot of it. They're well supplied with arms and support, and they probably have near as good connections as we do. The only difference between us and them is that we have the advantage of working on our home turf. We need to keep that advantage, and we do that by putting them down and keeping them down. We don't give them any quarter and we put our foot on their necks when they get out of line. They have to understand we're not just going to roll over, and we need to make sure we send a message about what happens when you go against the Family—when you go against us."

Bolan was surprised when every man in the room burst into applause, some even cheering. He hadn't really meant to give a speech, but nobody could have blamed him for getting into the part. It was something the Executioner did naturally in role camouflage. He inspired and commanded, no matter what the setting, and there was something in his nature that even now demanded the attention of these men.

They were different from him—so very different—and yet he could still set a command-and-control atmosphere.

"That all sounds good, Frankie," Donatto mouthed off again. "But just how do you suggest we do this?"

"By sending them the same message they sent us," Bolan said, snapping back. "Word has it these guys are going to be working tonight. We need to return the favor for San Francisco, and we need to do it now. There's no telling what they'll be able to do once they get this computer system going that they've been making us all pay for, and we can't just let what happened go by without making sure they understand what happens when you cross us."

"So you want us to risk sending in a bunch of our guys and blowing everything to hell?" Donatto asked.

Bolan fixed him with a level stare and replied, "Yeah, that's what I'm suggesting."

There was a long pause as the two men studied each other. Donatto's expression seemed almost like one of amusement, as if he were sizing up Bolan. He was, after all, probably the highest-ranking Mob member in that room, but he'd chosen to let others run the show. The reality was that he probably didn't know a whole hell of a lot about the New Islamic Front, and maybe he didn't care. It was entirely possible that Donatto was there to sniff around and see if he could get something out of the deal. The guy was a cutthroat opportunist, and Bolan didn't trust him one damn bit. Still, this is what he had to work with and he couldn't very well throw any offer for assistance back in their faces, or it would most definitely arouse suspicion.

Finally, Donatto looked around at the others and said, "I'm willing to commit ten of my best guys. What about the rest of you?"

It didn't take but a moment for the rest of them to nod among themselves, and Bolan was satisfied. The first part of his plan was working. Sure, the Mob fought with one another like ravenous wolves, but give them a common enemy and they would flock together putting "Family" honor first.

"So now that we're all in agreement," Donatto said, after the group had calmed, "how do you propose to do this?"

"I say the first thing we do is go to where we set up their systems and take care of business. We have to send a message." Bolan watched the faces and all seemed agreeable.

"Then what?" Gino asked.

Bolan's tone was cold and hard and determined. "And then we find the ones in charge of these bastards, and we cut out their hearts."

BOLAN FOUND AN EXCUSE to get away after the meeting broke, and after driving around the town to verify he wasn't followed, he found a pay phone near an abandoned warehouse and called Stony Man.

"It's me," he told Brognola. "How are things going?"

"Not good," the Stony Man chief replied, getting immediately down to business. "I'm afraid they're not good at all, Striker. Some members of the NIF snatched Rhatib, and in the process they killed a number of federal correctional officers as well as two U.S. Marshals."

Bolan's heart went out to the slain officers and their families. He knew what it meant to suffer that kind of loss. There were countless brave souls just like those federal officers, making the ultimate sacrifice to protect those who could not protect themselves. He knew their kind because he was their kind, and because he had fought beside them repeatedly. The worst part of such tragedies was that the majority of the country didn't know their names, and yet they were benefactors of their sacrifice.

"We have any leads?" Bolan asked.

"I decided to go through usual channels to conduct the actual investigation. Phoenix is handling something overseas right now, and I've got Able dealing with the protection of MacEwan's mother. That was part of the deal. But Barb will be working with the FBI in keeping up on any of their findings."

"So, you've got MacEwan's family covered but what about her? Is she safe?"

"Yes," Brognola replied. "We've got her tucked away in a safehouse, and she's working diligently with Bear to figure out what's happening with the network systems. I've get to tell you, she is one sharp lady."

"Agreed. So with Rhatib on the loose, where does that leave us?"

"Well, we might have an opportunity here if we exploit it," Brognola suggested. "We believe the NIF has some agents operating inside the country who are in fact remnants of your little visit to that mountain fortress in Afghanistan."

"How did you find this out?"

"It was actually Barb who picked up on it."

Yeah, that didn't surprise Bolan at all. There were few—*very* few—like Barbara Price. The woman had a knack for finding needles in haystacks, and it was this insight that had averted more potential disasters than anyone at Stony Man cared to count. While Price wasn't a field operative, she remained an invaluable part of the team as Stony Man's mission controller.

"About three days ago, a plane went down just off the D.C. coast. The Coast Guard was about to conduct a spot inspection of a yacht when the call came through, so they had to break off and head for the downed aircraft," the big Fed continued his explanation.

"Let me guess," Bolan interjected. "Members of the NIF were on that boat."

"Well, we don't have any proof but we *think* that's what happened," Brognola replied. "The Air Force's tracking systems were never able to confirm that any aircraft was in that area when it reportedly went down, and the Coast Guard team never found any wreckage."

"It does sound suspicious," Bolan said.

"We're still investigating, but we're not optimistic we'll find anything to suggest it was anything other than a decoy."

"And it's too elaborate to be a practical joke."

"Issuance of a false Mayday is no joke," Brognola said. "It's a federal offense and usually carries jail time. Which means the perpetrators of such a hoax cared little for any possible penalties they might face, or were extremely desperate to accomplish their true objectives. We'll keep on it and see if we can find that yacht."

"Good enough. But I'm still not sure about the ties to the group I took down in Afghanistan."

"That has to do more with Rhatib. Rhatib's father was killed during the liberation of Afghanistan by American forces, but apparently he has an uncle who was once part of the Taliban. He also held an honorary military rank as a colonel in Iraq's Republican Guard."

"What do we know about this guy?"

"His name is Umar Abdalrahman. His current status and location is unknown, unless we're correct about him possibly being here in the country now. He's on Homeland Security's most-wanted list. There's no telling how deep his involvement with the NIF goes, or what he's really responsible for."

"I think I could guess," Bolan replied dryly. "What about Lenzini's network?"

"You should know that Bear and the team managed to crack his security. Apparently, it wasn't as difficult as we'd thought it would be. But then again, it served its intended purpose by wasting a lot of precious time. Frankly, I'm afraid this news isn't any better than the last."

"What's going on?"

"We found everything from customer databases to inventory records of warehouses stocking entertainment media, such as books, CDs, and video games. Hell, the list is practically endless. The problem is that none of this data is valid. While on the surface it would appear that Lenzini's running nothing more than an Internet-based business, the reality is something else entirely. Bear's telling me it's all just a sham. It gets pretty technical, but what we know for a certain is that all of this data, when unencrypted using what's called assembly language, will actually do something. What we haven't yet figured out is how to decode it, and once we have, we don't know what it will do.

"But MacEwan was able to tell us that she thinks this proves a definite link to our theory about Malcolm Shurish being involved with NIF. We've got teams out searching for him right now. He hasn't reported to work all week at DARPA. I've had Justice keep a very tight lid on our suspicions of him and his culpability in all of this, so we don't send up any warning flags."

"Sounds like the right approach, Hal," the Executioner replied. "Chances are that he could be hacked into every federal information channel across the country and watching for any mention of his name."

"That was our assessment, as well," Brognola said. "I don't know how easy it's going to be to find him. MacEwan said something about having to shut down every system on the network, or having to shut down the source system. We think that explains Shurish's disappearance. He may be at the source system, ready to implement this code and bring the whole thing online."

"Is there any chance my destroying the network on a site-to-site basis will be enough?"

"MacEwan seems to think so," Brognola said, "but Bear believes we should have a backup plan. The thing that has us most concerned is the timing of it. We're not sure how long you have, and we know we need a failsafe plan in case the NIF implements this system before you're able to destroy the network."

"I've managed to get a few things cooking," Bolan said. "This wasn't the way I wanted to do it, but I don't see we have any choices. For whatever reason, Lenzini's people tried to smoke me in San Francisco. I neutralized Pescia's crew there, and now I'm in L.A."

"What's happening there?"

"This is one of the network sites, and according to the intelligence you gave me at my initial briefing, the NIF has people here working on the getting the system up and running fully. I plan to make sure that doesn't happen."

"It sounds to me like you've got things well in control, Striker."

"I appreciate the confidence, but this isn't going to be as easy at it sounds. The key to getting everyone in the Mafia to agree with you is to make them think it was their idea. That's worked so far, and I've managed to rally some pretty heavy hitters."

"Such as?"

"A guy named Ray Donatto, for one," Bolan said. "He's apparently quite well-respected out here on the West Coast."

"You mean well-feared," Brognola reminded him.

"Fair enough," Bolan conceded. "In any case, he's rallied some support for the cause, and I plan to use that to my advantage. I just need to be careful. I don't think he totally trusts me."

"You need to be careful no matter what, Striker. We can't afford to lose you."

"I wouldn't worry too much about that," Bolan replied. "I know eventually I'll go, but it won't be today."

"What time is this hit supposed to go down?" Brognola asked.

"Midnight, sharp, according to the plan. I figure the NIF will be in there working full tilt. Pescia tells me they were working on the systems during the night because they didn't want to draw attention."

Brognola sighed. "It's a sad idea, but I guess I can see how thirty or forty Middle Easterners operating out of an office building in the heart of Los Angeles would be fairly conspicuous."

"Yes, but the nice thing about the timing is that it will help me eliminate the risk of innocents getting in the way. I'll have to find some way to draw any security guards out of the line of fire."

"Any ideas yet on how you're going to do that?"

"Not a clue, but I'll come up with something."

"All right, well then I'd better let you get to it. Try to keep us informed."

"Understood."

"Good luck, Striker."

"Ditto. Out here."

Bolan clicked off the line and then checked his watch. He still had almost six hours before showtime. He hadn't really formulated a full plan yet, but he had some ideas he thought were pretty sound. Based on what Brognola had told him, he was running out of time. He had to make sure the job went off precisely here, and there were still the locations in Seattle to deal with, not to mention that he'd have to return to Boston and finish off Lenzini. And then there was the NIF to worry about, and the disappearance of Rhatib. There was only one certainty, and that was the numbers were ticking off. Time was no longer an issue, because the warrior didn't really have any.

Yeah, things weren't about to just heat up in Los Angeles—they were going to heat up across the whole country.

12

The building was tall and ominously foreboding, nestled in a seemingly abandoned area of downtown Los Angeles. Only a few lights dotted the front of the building, leaving the majority of the offices dark.

Bolan could tell that Pescia's intel was true, because many of the offices on the floor where Lenzini's sham business operated were lit, cutting a bright line through the otherwise darkened steel and glass facade. Within a very short time, that was about to change entirely. In fact, before the night was over, those offices would become dark, cold tombs for a great many of the enemy.

Bolan and Pescia sat in a van borrowed from one of the mobster's dealers, and watched the place carefully for any possible police activity. That was something the Executioner could definitely not afford at this point in the game; he could see how some poor overanxious rookie might start poking around the area and end up putting the warrior in a position of having to change his plans. Still, Bolan wasn't going to worry about it. He was confident this mission would come off as planned. They had been sitting there for nearly an hour and not a single squad car had passed through.

"You're kind of quiet, Frankie," Pescia said.

Bolan looked at the high-priced junk dealer and said, "Nothing to say."

"Are you nervous?"

"Not really," Bolan said with a shrug. "Are you?"

"I guess a little bit. I haven't done nothing like this for quite a long time. I got out of the business as a soldier because I don't really have a taste for killing. I mean, at least not like Donatto or any of his people. Now Ray, man, that guy *loves* to kill. Don't know what that's about, and never have understood it, but I do know he's got quite a reputation for it. They say he once—"

"Look, Gino," Bolan cut in, "nothing personal but I don't really give a crap what Donatto's done. All I care about is that everyone does their job tonight."

"Yeah, okay," Pescia replied uncertainly. "I understand, Frankie."

Bolan nodded and went back to watching the building, enjoying the silence as Pescia decided to shut up and smoke a cigarette. He was having a hard time sitting in the enclosed van, inhaling all of the smoke. The Executioner had chosen to kick the habit long ago, and while he didn't begrudge other smokers, it was hardly tolerable in the confines of the van. Bolan thought for a moment about complaining, but he opted against it. If it kept Pescia quiet and occupied, he didn't care if the guy chain-smoked both of them into a cancer ward. It didn't bother Bolan enough to distract him from watching for trouble.

In a sense, these kinds of activities in his war plan were like playing chess. There were moves and countermoves and having to constantly outthink the opposition. Not to mention the fact that the Mafia was an enemy with which to be reckoned.

It was Bolan's job to hold the savagery in check, and make sure only the enemy was the subject of it. Whether it was the New Islamic Front or the Mafia that ultimately fell this night, at least the warfare would be kept to those who were involved, and Bolan could get the innocents out unscathed.

He'd made a radical decision in dealing with the security guards. He was taking a big chance on this one, but he could only nut up and do it, and hope his risk paid off. Bolan wasn't just gambling with his own life, he was gambling with the lives of the security personnel who were posted at the desk in the lobby of the building. After making a few calls, Bolan also obtained information that there was a pair of roving guards, but they traveled together rather than moving through the building separately. So, it was a fifteen-story building with four guards—that meant he'd have to get the quartet together and do it quickly.

Bolan started to open the door but stopped when he felt Pescia grab his jacket. The Executioner turned a hard look on Pescia, and the guy winced in reflex action.

"Where are you going?" he asked.

Bolan smiled. "I'm going to handle those guards inside. Somebody has to do it."

"I thought we planned to take care of that when we went in."

"I've changed my mind."

Pescia snorted and shook his head. "Donatto's not going to like this."

"Donatto's not in charge here," Bolan replied, stabbing him in the chest with his finger. "You are. Now, you want to risk our guys or you want to let me go in ahead of them and do this sensibly?"

Bolan could see the wheels turning as Pescia thought furiously about it. He decided to take a different approach and closed the door so the interior light stopped illuminating them. "Listen, all one of those guys has to do is push a button. That's it, Gino, just push a button and it's all through. Now yeah, we will probably get to them before they can do that. But what if we don't? What if one of the guys blows it? We'll be done with this before it ever gets off the ground, and then the Arabs are going to know we're onto them and they'll lock down tighter than a drum, and we'll have *no* chance. And we'll both have outlived our usefulness to Don Lenzini. Is that what you want?"

Pescia finally shook his head. "No, you're right, Frankie. As usual. I got to tell you, I'm sure glad to have a stand-up guy like you around. This comes out good for us, Frankie, and I'm going to make you something. I'll make you bigger than Grano or my lead guy now."

Bolan nodded in way of thanks and then got out of the van and walked nonchalantly in the direction of the office building. He'd been wearing an overcoat, and in the darkness Pescia hadn't really noticed what he had underneath it. Bolan could only be thankful it was a cold time of year, otherwise such a get-up would have looked strange. The overcoat concealed his blacksuit and weaponry, including the Desert Eagle and Beretta. He also had the FNC folded and swinging beneath his right armpit, suspended on his shoulder by a strap.

The Executioner was girded for war, but he didn't know who the real enemy would be. On the one hand, it was possible that the syndicate's goons well outnumbered whatever minimal security the NIF had inside, possibly because they were relying on Lenzini to play straight with them and protect their interests. That was, after all, how he'd first encountered Gino Pescia at the Garden of Allah in D.C. The other possibility was that the NIF—distrustful of the Mafia—would have nothing short of an army protecting their investments. In either case, it promised to be a very dangerous encounter, and Bolan had to keep things balanced. He was the wild card, and while he didn't like the idea he knew there was little in the way of a choice.

As always, Bolan would do his duty no matter what the personal cost.

The Executioner reached the heavy, double plate-glass doors and rapped his knuckles heavily on one of them. Both guards behind the front security desk looked up simultaneously, surprise registering in their expressions. Obviously, they weren't used to someone knocking on the doors at that time of night. Bolan knew that there was only a slim chance they'd let him in, but he'd already calculated that into his plan.

One of the men leaned over the desk and touched something unseen, and the intercom just outside the door crackled to life. "Can I help you, sir?" the guard asked.

"Um, yes sir, my name is Matt Cooper, and I'm with Pro-Tech Office Cleaners. I'm doing a spot inspection on our people. They were supposed to call and let you know I was coming."

The guard looked puzzled for a moment, and then replied, "One moment, please."

An office building of that size had to maintain quite a cleaning crew, and it wasn't at all unusual for someone to do a spot check on those crews. Earlier that evening, after hanging up with Brognola, Bolan had contacted a number of cleaning services specializing in office maintenance. In doing so, he'd asked for references and he'd expended a considerable amount of change before someone had finally dropped the name of Lenzini's dot-com there in L.A. Then it was a simple matter of calling the security company and making them aware they would have a late-night visitor. Getting the forged credentials had been the least of his problems.

Stony Man had contacts everywhere, and could reach even into the most remote places and areas for assistance if required. That was the advantage of being backed by the most powerful political office in the world.

The guard tried to look as official as possible as he consulted with the second guard, and after a moment they nodded at each other in agreement. The intercom clicked on and the guard instructed Bolan to stand away from the door. A moment later, it swung open automatically and the warrior moved inside before either man had a chance to change his mind. Once he was past the vestibule he surrendered his forged credentials.

"Guess your company takes this stuff seriously," one guard said, making idle chitchat while the other took Bolan's identification and logged him in.

"Yes, sir," Bolan replied. "They're trying to improve customer service across the board."

"Did you get some kind of poor ratings or something?"

"I don't know," Bolan said with a mock shrug. "I was just recently hired by this company."

"Yeah, I was wondering why I'd never seen you before. Of course, that's not really surprising. Last time we had someone come out here from your company on one of these, was—" he scratched behind his ear and concluded "—well, hell, I can't even remember now."

Bolan tried to smile a disarming grin. "They don't let us out much either."

As the guard returned Bolan's forged credentials, his talkative partner shook his head and said, "Well, I'd bet they're paying you a hell of a lot better than they pay us. And you'll probably be stuck here…what, an hour?"

"If that," Bolan replied. As the Executioner reached inside his jacket in a show of returning his wallet, he wrapped his hand around the butt of the Beretta and brandished it before either of them could react. "Now let's play real nice with each other. Keep your hands where I can see them and step away from that desk."

"What the—"

"Just do it!"

Both guards got up, and Bolan moved quickly around the desk to place himself between them and their console. There were computer cameras everywhere, and the Executioner knew he wouldn't be able to take all of them out. He'd have to keep his face averted as much as possible.

"Listen carefully," Bolan said sharply. "I'm not here to hurt either of you."

"Could have fooled me!" the older, talkative guard exclaimed.

"I said listen," Bolan snapped. "In about two minutes, you're going to have the real enemy coming through the door. Now the only way I can keep you alive is to lock you away where you won't get in any trouble. But I also know that there are two more of you walking post on one of the upper floors. Where would they be now?"

"I don't know, and I sure as hell wouldn't tell you if I did," the younger guard replied.

"Sorry to hear that, because you may very well cost them their lives if you don't tell me."

The two guards exchanged uneasy glances, and Bolan let them chew on it for a second. He had to get them out of the line of fire, and he had to find the other two as well. The Executioner had gambled, risked that they would cooperate, but there wasn't a whole heck of a lot he could do about it if they chose not to help him. He wouldn't get another opportunity if he didn't sway them immediately.

"Time's up, gentlemen," Bolan said. "Which way is it going to be?"

One of the guards started to reach down and Bolan moved the pistol in his direction. The guard said quickly, "Easy, fella, I'm just reaching for my radio. I'm going to find out where they're at."

"Make sure that's all you do."

The guy nodded slowly and then snapped the radio off his belt and called one of the guards by his first name. He answered immediately, and it took only a moment for him to say they had just finished on the seventh floor and were headed up to the eighth. Bolan nodded to the guard that was enough information and waved them in the direction of the stairway. The guard looked at him with a funny expression, and Bolan could tell the older, paunchy guard wasn't quite prepared to climb eight flights of steps.

"You got some aversion to the elevators?" he asked Bolan.

The Executioner responded to the man's question with a frosty grin. He said, "The stairs will keep all of us alive."

The guard snorted. "Speak for yourself."

"Move out."

The two guards led Bolan to the stairwell and the men began to ascend. The younger guard and Bolan definitely had an easier time of it than the older, out-of-shape man. Bolan could hear him huffing and puffing by the time they'd reached the third landing, and the guy wanted to stop there and rest but Bolan wouldn't hear of it. He advised the man to keep going. By the time they had reached the sixth floor, Bolan knew he was out of time.

He stopped the guards and said, "You guys keep going until you find your friends, and then stay out of the way."

"What do you mean, 'stay out of the way'?" the older guard asked. "Of what?"

"Of the tenth floor, that's what. The guys who will be coming through here are only interested in one thing, and that's taking out the men at LenziNet, so you'd be well advised to steer clear of that floor. Once you've found your men, find a safe way to get back to the ground floor and get in touch with the police."

"Why are you doing this anyway? Don't you work for whoever these guys are?" the younger guard asked suspiciously.

"That's what they think, kid," Bolan said. "But they're in for a little surprise."

Bolan turned immediately and descended the stairs, emerging in the lobby just as the first of the Mafia men came through the door. They were an impressive-looking force, about twenty-five in all, including the ten crack troops promised by Donatto. Actually, Donatto's soldiers looked quite professional. They were dressed in black fatigue pants, black T-shirts and leather jackets. They were toting light hardware, mostly Uzis, but a couple were armed with AR-15s—civilian variants of the M-16—chambered for .223 hardball ammunition. Donatto came in right behind his men who were now fanning out, a .45-caliber pistol in his hand. Pescia was immediately on his heels.

"Where the fuck have you been?" Donatto asked Bolan.

"Taking care of the guards," Bolan replied. "And no disrespect, Donatto, but I don't answer to you. I work for Don Lenzini. Remember?"

Donatto sized up the Executioner a moment, looked as if he wanted to say something but changed his mind, then asked, "Where are the guards?"

Bolan grinned. "They're dead, and out of the way. That's all that's important. I did find out that our target's on the tenth floor, but we won't have a lot of time. We need to go in, do our business and get out."

"All right," Donatto replied with a nod. He turned toward his men who had secured the perimeter of the lobby and hollered, "Okay, listen up! I want you staggered into equal groups on board those elevators there! We want to make sure nobody passes us! Two of mine will stay behind to watch the lobby! Move out!"

The syndicate's soldiers obeyed immediately, moving toward the elevators as instructed. Bolan started to follow Donatto and Pescia, then stopped just as they were about to get aboard.

"Wait a minute, boys," Bolan said. "We've got nobody covering the stairway."

"Are you volunteering?" Donatto asked him.

"Yeah, but why don't you let Gino go with me."

"How about Gino should ride up, and I go with you," Donatto said.

"These guys are going to need someone with experience," Bolan said. He exchanged glances with Pescia and then added, "No offense, Gino, but you're not really that experienced at this. You said it yourself."

"Well, let's not spend a lot of time talking about it," Donatto said. "Fine, Gino go with Frankie here."

Pescia stepped off the elevator and turned to watch it close. As it did, Donatto smiled and said, "We'll try to leave you guys something."

Bolan waited until everyone had vacated the elevator banks then he headed back toward the lobby, Pescia in tow. He didn't have a lot of time, and while it would have seemed odd to most, it was the two men left behind to watch the lobby that posed the greatest threat to him. They had seen Bolan come in alive with the Mafia men. He had to make sure they never lived to tell that tale.

Bolan reached the lobby and found the two men sitting behind the desk where the security guards had been just minutes earlier. He shed his overcoat and produced the Beretta 93-R. The looks on their respective faces were ones of pure shock. Those looks were immediately followed by action as they clawed for their machine pistols, but it was entirely too late for that. Bolan took the first hood with a double-tap to the chest. The Beretta was whisper-quiet as the subsonic cartridges ratcheted from the ejection port, and the rounds blew holes in the guy's lungs. Bolan had the second one in sight before the body of the first had hit the floor, and a single round through the forehead ended any possible hope of resistance.

Bolan heard the hiss of a sudden, sharp intake of breath. He whirled on Pescia and put the smoking barrel inches from the guy's head.

"*You,*" Pescia finally stammered. "You were the one who killed our guys in San Fran."

"You guessed it, Gino," Bolan said.

"You really did want me to give that message to Lenzini."

"And you chose not to," Bolan said. "Your people cut their own throats in this deal."

Pescia's whole body began to shake as he said, "Oh yeah? And what did you do, Frankie, eh? You played judge and jury."

Pescia lunged at Bolan.

The Executioner passed judgment.

13

San Francisco, California

Serge Grano stood next to Lorenz Trabucco and the rest of his boys, and shook his head with great remorse.

The motel was nothing but ashes, burned to the ground, and the smell of charred materials was powerful. It wouldn't be long before they got people out to clean up the mess, but Grano was happy he'd had the opportunity to see this before that time. It fired him up, and gave him the added fuel he needed to find who was responsible for the deaths of so many of their people. They were still trying to identify some of the bodies, since only a few were outside the motel and the rest had been trapped inside by the fire.

Damn, Gino Pescia! Grano thought. That son of a bitch had put them out here like lambs to slaughter. If he'd had a problem with Don Lenzini's handling of the Arabs, he should have come to Grano and spoken up. He shouldn't have turned tail and run like some chickenshit weasel, and tried to come out to California and hide behind the skirts of his club dancers. Hadn't Don Lenzini always been good to them, and treated all of them like his own sons? It was shameful!

"Hey, boss," Trabucco said. "Who do you think did this?"

Grano didn't answer; he'd barely heard Trabucco. Grano was almost a hundred percent sure who had rained such death and destruction on their people: Frank Lambretta. What Grano saw here was too close to what he'd seen of what was left of the hitters he sent to finish Lambretta at the hotel. Hell, he'd *wanted* to trust Lambretta. After all, the guy had a great reputation as a loyal soldier, but apparently that was all talk. For all they knew, Lambretta was working for the Feds.

That was the most likely possibility. The stories Grano had heard so far were disturbing. There had been talk of this mystery man who fought like a devil and used automatic weapons and high explosives. The forensics reports coming from the police labs in downtown San Francisco were telling quite a tale. Grano was certain he'd seen and heard references to military-like weaponry such as assault rifles firing fully automatic, and explosive devices that included both incendiary and fragmentation grenades. Grano knew that kind of stuff came at a price, and he wasn't completely convinced that Lambretta had those kinds of connections. Still, the guys he'd sent to wipe out Lambretta had died under very similar circumstances, and thus far they hadn't heard anything from the guy.

Whatever the story, the top bull in the Lenzini crime Family was pretty sure that Lambretta wasn't on their side, and he was also convinced the guy was anything but loyal. It was possible "Loyal" Frankie-boy was actually under the employ of a competing Family. While the majority of syndicate businesses tried to work together these days, it was still an environment of territories and competition. The Families had moved away from being "Families" in the true sense of the word. Less credit was given for bloodlines and more toward those capable of doing the job. That idea had solidified many of their holdings across both domestic and foreign operations, but every once in a while someone tried to throw a wrench into the works.

It wasn't that Grano agreed with Don Lenzini's decision to join the New Islamic Front. He didn't trust the Arabs any more than he did the Irish or Hispanics. Still, his loyalty was first and always to the Family, and that meant he obeyed the orders of whoever was in power at the time. He remained loyal and he took care of the Family business because the Family took care of him. It was just that simple.

Grano, having forgotten about Trabucco, suddenly turned and looked at the enforcer. Trabucco was a wannabe, no question there, but he had guts and heart, and those were enough. Now, if he could just find some brains, he would be a half-decent soldier, and maybe even good enough to replace Grano one day. In either case, Grano knew that he had a much better chance than old man DeLama's kid, although he knew how protective Don Lenzini was of his friend's son. He could still hear his boss telling him that nothing was to happen to DeLama—absolutely nothing!

"What did you say, Lorenz?"

"I asked who you thought did this to our people," Trabucco said.

Grano shook his head, spared Ape a look and then replied, "I don't know, for sure, but I'm guessing it was either one of our West Coast competitors or Frankie Lambretta."

Trabucco didn't look as if he had anything intelligent to say in response to that. That was good, because Grano didn't really want to hear it anyway. The next step for them was to find Lambretta. He and the rest of his men headed for the car, and soon they were on the freeway.

"Where do you want to go now, boss?" Ape asked him.

Grano hadn't said ten words to the poor guy since they'd arrived in San Francisco, and he felt bad about it, but that was life. He hated this miserable weather—which was rainy and chilly this time of year—and he especially didn't like having to ride around with a busload of incompetents like they had now. Well, not entirely incompetent. Trabucco and DeLama left a lot to be desired, but Maxim and Huffman had proved themselves pretty competent guys.

"I'm not sure yet. We need to go to Gino's club and see if we can find out where the bastard split to. I swear, Ape, if he ran out on us with Lambretta, I'm going to fucking skin both of them alive. You hear me?"

"I hear you, boss."

"Hey, Serge," Trabucco chimed in, only irritating the head enforcer more. "What did the old man say about us losing that government broad? Is he pissed at us?"

"What do you think, Lorenz?" Grano answered. "Of course he's pissed at you. He gave you one simple job, just one simple job, and you dicked it up. Now, you think Don Lenzini's going to be happy about that?"

Trabucco's voice was lame and muted coming from the back of the six-seat, luxury SUV. "No, I don't suppose."

"You're damn right you don't suppose!"

Grano was losing his temper, but he didn't give a damn at that moment. He had to be tough on these guys, or they would get out of control and never learn anything and then when he was gone they'd get the old man smoked in a heartbeat. Except for Ape; he wouldn't let anything like that happen as long as he was still breathing. Then again, Alfonse was one hell of a good soldier, but he wasn't all that bright, and to be a chief enforcer you had to be pretty smart.

"Now there's a way you can make it up to him," Grano told them. "You guys can show me your stuff. If we catch up…no, *when* we catch up to Gino and this Lambretta guy, we're bound to have some trouble. You guys show your stuff, and do the right thing, and all will be forgotten. I can promise you that."

"We'll do well, boss. We promise." Trabucco looked at the others and added, "Isn't that right, boys?"

They just mumbled and nodded their agreement, although Maxim was—as usual—out like a light with his intermittent snoring becoming louder by the minute.

Grano smiled and shook his head ever so slightly. Well, he should let the big boy get his beauty rest. He was going to need Maxim when they caught up to Lambretta. He figured if they were on the square, they'd be glad to see the crew. And if not, well, then there would be trouble. Grano wasn't too worried about it—Pescia and Lambretta wouldn't stand much of a chance. These were six fairly experienced guys, except maybe for DeLama, and all of them had been in their share of scrapes. If nothing else they'd win by sheer numbers. The only thing Grano hoped was that he was wrong about Lambretta's involvement in what they'd just seen at that motel.

Maybe, just maybe, killing Lambretta wouldn't be so easy after all.

Los Angeles, California

MACK BOLAN COULD HEAR the first sounds of autofire as he reached the eighth-floor landing.

With the guards neutralized downstairs, and Gino Pescia dead, that left the Executioner with only one floor and one set of targets. In order to keep safe any other innocents still in the building, the warrior knew he'd have to keep things contained to the tenth floor. That meant he'd have to cover any routes of escape, which included stairwells and elevators, as well as individual offices where they could hide. And he'd have to do it all by himself.

Yeah, the odds were pretty much in the enemy's favor. As usual.

Bolan vaulted the stairs, making it to the tenth floor in less than fifteen seconds. He pushed through the door leading into a long, narrow hallway. At one end were the elevators, probably the same ones Donatto's team had ridden since they were being guarded by a trio of Mafia hard guys. The men turned at the sound of Bolan's entrance and he waved at them. They started to turn their weapons in his direction, but then the leader called them off, obviously remembering that they would have men covering the stairs.

The guys started to turn their attention back to the action ahead of them and that's when Bolan seized the advantage. The Executioner dropped to one knee, pressed the stock of the FNC against his shoulder, aligned his sights on the threesome and squeezed the trigger. The hallway was immediately filled with a cacophony of screams and autofire as Bolan did a full-burn number on them. The area where they stood was filled with 5.56 .45 mm NATO slugs, and the trio fell under Bolan's marksmanship.

The Executioner sprinted down the hallway and pressed the buttons to call all three elevators. He crouched, listening as the firefight continued inside the main offices. From his vantage point, he couldn't yet see the aftermath of the battle, but he knew it wouldn't be pretty. It sounded as if Donatto's men were unleashing hellfire on their perceived enemy, and that was just fine with Bolan. If he could keep them occupied a minute longer, he'd have them just where he wanted them.

The first of the elevator doors opened, and Bolan dragged one of the bodies into it, providing a barricade that would prevent the door from closing entirely. He then got inside the elevator and reached into the small satchel at his waist. He retrieved three one-pound sticks of C-4, which were taped to one another, and primed them with a wireless detonator. Bolan repeated these actions for the remaining pair of elevators and then changed to a fresh magazine.

Bolan stepped into the area that looked onto the main offices. It was wide open, although each area was divided by prefab walls and desks that formed individual cells, or cubicles. Bolan began to move through the winding maze of structures, looking for the first signs of conflict. He found it after only two turns, emerging on the backside of two syndicate troops being held at bay by what could only be NIF soldiers.

Bolan had fought against the New Islamic Front's people before, and he knew them when he saw them. There were four of them, positioned in staggered formation, two of them firing from an office space at the far end while the other two held positions in neighboring cubicles branching off an intersecting throughway.

The Executioner didn't wait for an invitation. He ducked back in the intersecting row he'd traversed, yanked an incendiary grenade from his harness webbing and pulled the pin. Bolan then rose to full height, stepped around the corner and sprayed the area where the two Mafia antagonists were hiding. Both men shouted with surprise as Bolan's rounds found their respective marks. The pair died with little fanfare.

Bolan stopped and waved at the NIF soldiers who were now completely unsure of what had happened, or the identity of their savior who stood there like a black angel of death. Nonetheless, they lowered their guard and exposed themselves. The Executioner started to walk toward them, holding his weapon in a nonthreatening manner. He then made a show of stopping at one of the guards and reaching out of sight. Bolan released the spoon on the grenade. He had, at most, three seconds before letting it fly and in that time he stood, looked at the grenade, shrugged, and then tossed it toward the still befuddled terrorists.

The bomb more closely resembled a can of hairspray than a grenade as it sailed toward them, and the guy to whom Bolan had tossed the grenade thoughtlessly reached out to catch it. The man had barely completed a full turn of it in his hand before it exploded, but by that time Bolan was now behind adequate cover. The TH3 white phosphorous immediately incinerated most of the flesh off the terrorist's body, and the exploded molten iron leaped across to envelope the flesh

of his comrades as well. Flames erupted from the unlucky terrorist's clothing, and he was immediately engulfed in flames.
Screams of horror, pain and shock were audible even above
the continuous gunfire throughout the rest of the offices, and
the first terrorist illuminated the area as he staggered around,
now little more than a human torch.

Bolan put mercy rounds in all four terrorists before continuing his search for other targets.

There was a sudden lull in the firing, probably the result
of the smoke and stench of burning human flesh that had
begun to fill the surrounding area. Moments later, the autofire started up again, and Bolan emerged onto another
throughway to find the NIF had the upper hand on this one.
Two NIF terrorists were kicking a Mafia hard guy on the
ground, and intermittently clubbing him with the stocks of
their rifles. They were so seemingly occupied with beating
their quarry to death that they didn't notice the Executioner
was now practically on top of them.

Bolan yanked the .44-caliber Desert Eagle from its holster and fired one shot for each. Both rounds connected, the
first one exploding the closer NIF terrorist's heart, while the
other collapsed the spine of his comrade with bone-crunch-
ing force, taking some of his intestines with it on exit. The
men collapsed, and the Mafia guy looked up, suddenly surprised that his torment had stopped. He looked up to see
Bolan standing over him.

"Oh, shit!" the Mob guy said. "Am I glad to see *you!*"

"Yeah," Bolan said as he raised the Desert Eagle and put
a bullet through the guy's head.

The Executioner holstered his weapon and continued
down that path in a crouch, the FNC held battle-ready. So far,
he'd only eliminated three on this floor, and counting the two
in the lobby along with Pescia, that left maybe a dozen or so.
It didn't take him long to reduce that number, when he hap-

pened on a quartet of Donatto's soldiers, all deceased. It looked like the NIF's resistance had been much heavier than expected.

Bolan's sixth sense suddenly triggered an alarm, and he turned and dropped in time to avoid being ventilated by a hailstorm of bullets. He crawled to an area of cover behind a filing cabinet and then rolled into a kneeling position. He leveled the FNC on the top of the waist-high cabinet, sighted on the closest of his targets and squeezed the trigger. The thin batting and plywood of the prefab dividers was no match for military-grade ammunition. Material and wood splinters exploded and lodged in the terrorist's face, evoking a shout of surprise. He rolled away in a natural desire to avoid death, but instead that was what he found. Bolan shot him twice through the top of the head.

The other two began to press forward, opening up with a continuous stream of autofire. Still, their timing was off and Bolan could tell he was dealing with completely inexperienced soldiers when firing from one gun ceased, followed by another a moment later. Both of his opponents had expended their ammunition almost simultaneously.

Bolan decided to deal with that by the easiest tactic possible, and that was heavy explosives. The soldier yanked a smoker from his harness, as well as an M67 fragmentation grenade packed with HE. Bolan removed the pins from both, but let the smoker fly first. He heard the grenade hit the floor, the yelling and uncertainty as the terrorists attempted to escape, and then he could hear it explode and the unmistakable hissing as smoke began to fill the room. Bolan released the M67 by leaving the cover of the cabinet for a moment and rolling the grenade down the walkway. He rolled back to his original position to insure he wouldn't fall victim to any fragments. The concussion alone rocked the area, and Bolan could smell the cordite and expended comp-B as the HE ignited. Flaming air whooshed past him as the grenade did its intended work.

In the aftermath of the shock wave, Bolan rose and took only a moment to survey the destruction. Bits and chunks of wrecked furniture and computer equipment lay everywhere, and one of the two terrorists was motionless. The last other had been left screaming and writhing on the ground, his body filled with superheated fragments of metal and wood. As Bolan moved past, he used the FNC to pump a few rounds into him, thereby ending his misery.

Bolan nearly walked into a group of Mafia soldiers that came around the corner, their weapons held at ready. The group was led by Ray Donatto. The mobster took one look at the destruction and a small, cruel smile played at his lips.

"Holy shit, Frankie, you do damn good work!"

"Yeah, whatever," Bolan said. "What's left of these guys?"

"Nothing," Donatto said. "We eradicated all of the bastards, but we lost a few of our own doing it."

"Yeah," Bolan replied, trying to act grim and saddened. He waved in the general direction from which he'd come and said, "I've seen nothing but dead bodies so far."

"It's okay," Donatto said, looking at his remaining men for approval. "They'll be remembered by the Family for eternity."

The men nodded and grumbled their agreement.

"So will we if we don't get out of here," Bolan reminded them. "You head for the elevators and I'll be right behind you."

"Where are you going?"

"Check for any survivors."

"But we already—"

"Ray, you want to take the chance of somebody being alive?" Bolan asked, cutting him off. "You want somebody talking to the Arabs, or worse, somebody talking to Don Lenzini or the cops before we're *finito?*"

Donatto looked like he'd been slapped, and Bolan realized he'd made a mistake in talking down to the guy in front of his men. Still, he knew in about a minute or two that it wouldn't matter.

"Now you go ahead, and I'll be right behind you."

"Hey, before you go," Donatto said, "where the hell is Gino?"

"He's dead. A straggler got him on the stairs. Son of a bitch took a bullet for me." Bolan forced a grin, adding, "Can you believe it?"

"I'll be damned," Donatto replied. He looked at Bolan and said, "I can't let you go it alone then. You need backup. My guys will head for the elevators and we'll search together."

Suspicion settled in Bolan's gut, but he knew it wouldn't do any good to argue. If he'd offered any resistance, Donatto would have suspected something. He didn't have any choice. Donatto had him pegged and anything other than accepting his offer would compromise him. He couldn't afford to let the cat out of the bag. Not yet…not with so much at stake.

14

"All right," Bolan said. "You're on."

Donatto turned to his men. "Get to the elevators and get the hell out of here. No, wait! Take the stairs."

"I wouldn't," Bolan said. "Most likely the cops will be here pretty damn quick and the stairs will take too long."

Donatto thought about a moment and nodded. "You're right. Take the elevators."

Bolan added, "We'll be right behind you."

The two moved off in the direction of the other offices while Donatto's men headed for the elevators. Bolan could only hope that the signal device inside his pocket would set off the C-4 at any sort of distance. He figured it wouldn't be a problem, although there might be a slight delay in the signal getting to it. The wizardry of Hermann "Gadgets" Schwarz wasn't to be underestimated, hadn't ever been underestimated, and Bolan wasn't about to start now.

That left the Executioner with only one other problem: he had to find a way to get rid of Donatto. The guy was behind him now, refusing to lead, and Bolan hadn't wanted to risk a firefight with a dozen of Donatto's hoods. He noticed that Donatto was keeping him at a disadvantage, and Bolan was beginning to wonder if the guy suspected something. So far, everybody around Bolan had ended up dead. The Executioner wasn't naive enough to believe his dumb luck would hold out forever. Good skills kept a soldier alive; intuition kept a soldier alive; and sometimes even destiny, a fate ordained by some higher power, kept a soldier alive. But reliance on luck alone would get a soldier killed quicker than anything else, except maybe underestimating the opposition.

The Executioner had learned these lessons the hard way, and he had also learned that when a guy had a gun at his back—even one who might think he was an ally—it was definitely *not* the time to risk a sucker play. Something told Bolan that it wasn't time to kill Donatto yet.

They continued through the offices, each splitting away to search more quickly and efficiently, and Bolan kept a constant vigil on his watch. As they rounded a far corner in the hallway, they found themselves heading toward the elevators, and Donatto's men were just off-loading the last of the human corpses Bolan had left as a time-delay mechanism. Donatto started to rush toward the men as they disappeared one by one onto the elevator, moving past Bolan in the process and affording the Executioner an opportunity.

Bolan reached into his pocket, retrieved the detonator, thumbed back the protective cover and pushed the button. The elevator area erupted into a ball of flame as the powerful plastique exploded under the heat and pressure of the blasting caps. Pieces of bodies, including arms, legs and heads, flew in every direction. Fire ignited the carpets and immediately began to crawl up the walls, and as the smoke roiled and the heat reached the fire sensors, the sprinklers started raining water on that zone.

Bolan trotted forward and grabbed Donatto's arm. He was trying to get up after being knocked to the ground by the shock wave. Bolan urged him on with a few, well-chosen but harsh words. Donatto was visibly upset by watching his men being blown to bits, but the Executioner simply pushed him into the stairwell, careful to insure the guy didn't collapse on his rubbery legs.

As they reached the landing below, Bolan suddenly noticed the reason for Donatto's strange behavior. It wasn't shock. There was a large piece of metal protruding from his head. Bolan couldn't tell what it was in the dimly lit stairwell, but he could see that it was embedded deeply in Donatto's skull, which meant—for all practical purposes—that it might even be lodged in a portion of the guy's brain.

In either case, as Bolan continued to assist Donatto down the steps, the effects of the injury were taking a toll. He was acting almost as if he was drunk, stumbling along as they continued to descend the steps. His movements were jerky and uncoordinated, and it took all of the Executioner's strength to hold on to the guy and maintain his own balance.

After what seemed like hours, but was really only a matter of minutes, Bolan reached the first floor with Donatto. He moved into the lobby, practically dragging Donatto's corpselike form along with him, sweeping the area with the muzzle of the FNC. There were no challengers, but Bolan knew it wouldn't be long before help arrived. He could see the flashes of light from the first police and fire vehicles arriving on the scene. Well, he thought, at least the security guards had been diligent in following his instructions to get help, and in staying out of his way during this mission.

Bolan turned and headed toward the rear of the building. He remembered seeing the alleyway, and he knew that Donatto's car was parked one street over. It wouldn't be difficult to get away unseen, provided that he didn't have to drag his burden the entire way.

Bolan nearly lost his balance under Donatto's weight, and he finally had to stop and ease the limp form to the linoleum. The capo looked up into Bolan's eyes, that cruel half smile playing on his lips as he wheezed and gasped, his brain trying to force him to continue breathing even though it was probably being flooded with blood. Yeah, the guy was dying a slow death.

"You aren't really part of the Family," Donatto said quietly, "are you?"

Bolan saw no reason to deny it at this point, and he shook his head.

"I—I knew it," Donatto finally managed to get out, gasping. "I…knew…it…"

The man died.

Bolan rose and put this thing from his mind. He'd accomplished the second stage of his mission, so he was halfway there. Next, he had to neutralize the major electronics site that provided communications throughout all of Lenzini's networks. That would wrap up his activities on the West Coast. He would then go back and deal with Lenzini.

Bolan was uneasy about the NIF and their *real* plans in this. In fact, he was more concerned about that than anything Lenzini was cooking up. Everything had seemed a bit too easy to this point. While he trusted his plan as the best one for going against the syndicate, he wasn't sure the same tactics would work with the NIF. It was one thing to get Mafia guns itching for a fight to believe that they were being betrayed by a foreign terrorist group, but it was quite another to make the NIF think they had anything to fear in a converse fashion. After all, the NIF had operated within American borders for some time with impunity, and the Executioner wasn't about to let that continue. One way or another, he would have to stop them. Even if he managed to destroy the alliances between Lenzini and whoever was running the show for the terrorists, it didn't mean the dangers were over; in fact, they would have just begun.

Bolan trusted Brognola and the genius of Aaron Kurtzman, and he was wholly confident in MacEwan's technical abilities, as well. Still, there were times when a soldier couldn't rely on the tenacity and skills of others, but instead had to turn to something deeper and more personal.

Yeah. The Executioner was taking the war straight to the

enemy. And they would find, when he was knocking on their door, there was no place to run.

Washington, D.C.

COLONEL ABDALRAHMAN had heard enough.

He'd started pacing when the reports first came through that there had been trouble at their base in Los Angeles, but now he was hearing of death tolls and the words "total destruction" being whispered on the breaths of many of his most trusted men. This wasn't good. It wasn't good for the morale of the New Islamic Front's soldiers, and it wasn't good for the success in their operations.

Abdalrahman had barely left Rhatib and Shurish since returning from his meeting with Lenzini. During the aftermath of their tragedy, he watched them as they worked furiously to reroute some of the systems to other locations. Primary data was being sent to the large communications network they had operating by remote satellite at an abandoned warehouse facility on the outskirts of Seattle, and the remainder was being handled by a location somewhere near Washington. That was a secret location, by Shurish's design. That, coupled with Shurish's insistence that they move their operations from the relative safety of his home in the foothills to this abandoned factory near the Potomac, had infuriated Abdalrahman.

Shurish, who allegedly did not know of the location of the Seattle base, had said it was best that nobody possess knowledge of the location of every key site in the operation. This way, if someone was captured and under torture or pain of death they decided to talk, the system could not be brought to its knees. While it sounded good, Abdalrahman believed that Shurish was simply guaranteeing his safety. Shurish could not take any *real* credit for the system, since it had almost solely been designed and built by Rhatib's genius, but he had assisted in some respects. Shurish's contacts within the American government had provided the gateway for the NIF to establish an operational foothold inside the country.

Their initial plan to control American defense systems using Carnivore, a tool used by the FBI to spy on its own citizens, had failed, largely in part to the interference of the man called Cooper and the American bitch who had worked for Shurish at DARPA. As soon as the Americans discovered the leak, they shut it down. Still, by striking a deal with the American organized crime syndicate, they would be able to control American defenses on a large enough scale that it would spell doom for their most hated enemy.

But Abdalrahman suspected none of it would come to pass if they did not determine what enemy was striking out at them, and attempting to destroy the system. Those were the answers he needed, those were the answers he'd ordered Shurish to get, and he had tired of waiting.

"Well?" he finally said, stopping his pacing and coming to stand over Shurish's shoulder.

The scientist was studying a computer screen, beads of sweat visible on his skin as they glowed in the light of the CRT. "I'm still tallying the reports, Umar."

"Bah!" Abdalrahman spit. He reached past Shurish, grabbing hold of the CRT, and with an angry shout he tossed the monitor across the room.

A heavy silence fell on everyone, broken only by the rasping of Abdalrahman's breath. His face was visibly red, and he could feel the flush. His heart beat rapidly. He was fed up with Shurish and the weak-minded simpleton's feeble excuses.

"You are supposed to be one of the best!" Abdalrahman exclaimed. "You are supposed to be intelligent and dependable, but instead you whine and fret about your day, wringing your hands! I have grown tired of it!"

The expression on Shurish's face became apoplectic, as he was now so angered by Abdalrahman's outburst that he looked as if he wanted to reach out and strangle the man barehanded. "And you are *supposed* to be some brilliant, military tactician but you cannot seem to stop one man. *One man,* Umar! Do you think me so weak that I could not kill a man with my own hands were I pushed to that? Yet we ask you to do one simple thing! We ask you to provide us security, to protect us from this man, and you cannot even do that! *I* stood within inches of this man, and risked my life by allowing that bomb to go off!"

"You risked nothing!" Abdalrahman shouted, stepping back and letting his hand hover over his pistol holster.

The movement wasn't lost on Shurish. "Oh, so you want to kill me? Then kill me! Where will your precious system be then, eh? Tell me that, if you can, Umar! Tell me all about how this system is going to work if I'm dead!"

It was taking everything in his being not to pull his weapon and shoot Shurish in his bitter, screwed-up face. Ah, yes, he would have loved nothing better than to blow a hole in the man's forehead. Still, he knew he needed Shurish, that he could not risk the operation, and Shurish knew it too.

"So," a quiet voice said. Both men turned to face Rhatib as he added, "It has finally come to this."

Abdalrahman slowly moved his hand away from his gun. While his nephew wasn't squeamish, the soldier certainly didn't want to expose him to such naked violence unnecessarily.

"Do you think we will succeed while at each other's throats?" Rhatib asked.

Abdalrahman could barely hold back the tears of pride that suddenly came to his eyes. His nephew—his beloved Rhatib—had emerged as a voice of maturity, calm and reason. It was almost too much for his soul to bear. He'd always found his nephew to be immature in a number of ways, but now Rhatib was talking like a true man.

"That is what they would like us to do, "Rhatib said. "They would like us to forgo our sense of duty and honor to our country, to our religion, to our people. The Americans would love nothing better than to see us destroy ourselves, so that all they have to do is step in and collect the spoils of our own bloodshed. This is the time we must band together, my brothers. This is the time that we must work with one another to accomplish our goal.

"Shurish, you must work with me, so that we can insure nothing goes wrong at the time we must strike. You must not let things worry you, particularly if those are things that are none of your concern. You should be concentrating on your work."

He turned to Abdalrahman. "And you, Uncle…"

"I—"

"Please," Rhatib demanded, looking down and closing his eyes as he dropped his hand as a signal for silence. He then looked Abdalrahman in the eyes and said, "This is our chance to avenge all of our brothers, and all of those who have sacrificed before us. I came to realize while imprisoned by the Americans that each of us has a destiny, and if we are to succeed and join our brothers with Allah, then we must be prepared to do whatever is necessary to accomplish that destiny. I have prayed for you, and I have discovered that your destiny is clouded. It is clouded by this man they call Cooper. I have seen this man firsthand, seen the demons in his eyes, and I can affirm here and now that we will *not* be able to claim complete victory until he is dead."

Rhatib stepped forward, and Abdalrahman thought his heart would burst. He was full of pride. His nephew reached one, thin arm around his uncle, kissed him on both cheeks in ceremonial fashion, and whispered, "It is your destiny to destroy this man. Fulfill your destiny."

Abdalrahman stepped back and looked into his nephew's eyes. He knew what this meant. He would have to fulfill his destiny, just as Rhatib had said, and he knew it could mean his death. Abdalrahman knew, just from what he'd heard and seen of this American, that Cooper was extremely dangerous, and not to be underestimated. Nonetheless, he knew that they would never have peace—just as Rhatib had prophesied—as long as Cooper was alive. The man would not give up. He would continue to hound their steps day and night, and haunt Abdalrahman's dreams, as he had so many times over this past week, until they killed him.

"You understand what you're asking me to do?" he asked Rhatib.

Rhatib nodded.

"And you also understand that I might not come back from this, my destiny?"

Rhatib nodded again, but this time there was a bit of sadness that fell upon his expression. "I also understand that you will not know true peace until he is dead, and you have accomplished your mission as Allah wills it."

Abdalrahman believed it was Allah's will that he do this. He also believed he would not have to actively search for Cooper. If it was his true destiny, the man would practically fall from the sky and right into his pistol sights, and he would avenge the deaths of many of his men, and right all of the wrongs that had occurred at Cooper's hand in Afghanistan.

Abdalrahman turned to Shurish. "You are right, of course. I owe you an apology. I have not accomplished my duties as I should have, and it is time for me to do so. From what you know, who do you think destroyed the complex in Los Angeles?"

"From the evidence found there, it was most like competing factors in the syndicate. Probably an old grudge that Lenzini's people felt they needed to settle. We cannot be sure. However, we also have heard reports that a similar attack occurred on their people in San Francisco."

"Similar in what manner?"

"If I had to compare them, I would say they were *tactically* similar," Shurish said.

"Which means, perhaps, the same source of the attacks."

"Precisely."

"So it would not make sense that any of Lenzini's competition would kill their own."

"Also true," Shurish replied.

"That means that someone is manipulating the situation, and that someone is probably Cooper," Abdalrahman said, and felt a grin come to his lips. He turned to his nephew and asked, "Where do you think he will go?"

"I think he will go where he most believes another attack will count."

Abdalrahman nodded. Of course, it made perfect sense. And so, the colonel would go there as well. And at last—at long last—he would fulfill his destiny.

15

Los Angeles, California

His crew was hot on the trail of their quarry, and Serge Grano could sense it.

Grano had just hung up his cell phone after having a long conversation with the old man, and he was considering what their next move should be. Somebody had called for a raid on LenziNet, one of their front operations put in place for the Arabs, and now it was a shambling ruins. Their people were dead, and some of the hitters were identified as being from Ray Donatto's crew. Gino Pescia's body was also found. The guy had been shot through the head execution style, and Donatto was believed to have been killed by fragments from terrible explosions at the building in downtown L.A.

That left only one person unaccounted for—Frankie Lambretta. Again, Lambretta was nowhere to be found. That had Grano deeply disturbed. This time, the hit had been perpetrated by a competing Family, but there was only one way they could have known about the site, and that was Gino Pescia. He was the only one—outside of Don Lenzini and a few others—who knew that place in Los Angeles even existed.

What the hell is going on here? Grano wondered.

Grano had to admit that someone else was pulling all the strings on this one. But he had been in this business a long time, and he knew a setup when he saw one. He was almost convinced that this was just too elaborate to be a true conspiracy. Unless there was a part of the story he was missing. Grano was guessing that Lambretta was the one who could fill in that piece of the puzzle.

On the one hand, it was possible that the Arabs had betrayed them. It was true that they had the manpower and equipment, if not the balls, to go after their people in San Francisco and make it look the competition. That would have then explained the hit in Los Angeles. Obviously, after the Arabs wiped out the private little army Gino had been building for himself in San Francisco, he went to Los Angeles and recruited the competition—competition that profited from Pescia's drug peddling—to seek payback for the slaughter.

The whole thing seemed pretty far-fetched, but supposing it was possible, that still didn't explain for Lambretta's disappearance. All others were accounted for, and if there had been survivors, Grano figured Lambretta should have been found among the dead. The guy wasn't that good—hell, *nobody* was that good. And if, in fact, Lambretta had survived, then he was one tough bastard, in which case he could outfox all of them and should be considered a threat to the Family.

But Lenzini saw it otherwise. He felt it was possible that Lambretta had escaped by the skin of his teeth, or after the hit he'd gone into hiding and had nothing to do with what had happened in San Francisco or Los Angeles. Lenzini was assuming that their true enemies were either members of the religious fanatics or a competing Family. Frankly, Grano wasn't really buying either theory.

"Hey, boss," Trabucco said. "What's the story here? Are we going to war?"

"Don't get your panties in a knot over this, Lorenz," Grano replied harshly. "Nobody's going to war with nobody yet. We need to find Frankie Lambretta, and we need to do it quick.

But Don Lenzini wants us to watch our asses, because he thinks that *if,* and I mean if, the Arabs have betrayed us, we might be next on the hit list."

Joey DeLama spoke up, his heavy Bronx accent evident. "Mr. Grano, do you really buy this shit about the rags turning on us?"

Grano saw an opportunity here to spout his own views. He wouldn't normally have done so, out of respect for the old man's wishes, but he figured it was okay since he'd been asked. After all, what could it hurt, right? He was entitled to have his opinion, and that opinion could disagree with Don Lenzini's, just as long as he did his job.

"No, I think it's bullshit, Joey," Grano replied. "I think that this Lambretta has some explaining to do, and that's why I say we find him before we start jumping to conclusions. But that's a good question, Joey. The rest of you guys could actually learn something from this kid."

"So where do we go now, Serge?" Trabucco asked.

"I think we should pay a visit to Gino's pad," Grano replied. "He thought we didn't know about his place, but he stupidly put the rent in the name of one of his girlfriends, thinking we didn't know nothing about her, either. Except for the fact that Gino was loudmouth, and he bragged so many times at his club about doing this hot babe in L.A., and before long he was throwing her name around to everyone who'd listen to him."

"You think we'll find Frankie there?" Ape asked.

"I don't know," Grano replied truthfully, "but at least it's a place to start."

DESPITE THE FACT that soap and water had washed away the stench of gun powder, blood and smoke, one odor seemed to cling continuously to the Executioner: death. It was probably one he would never be able to fully wash away; at least, not as long as he had a duty to perform in this War Ever-lasting.

Nonetheless, Mack Bolan felt almost relieved as he stepped from a very hot shower at Pescia's apartment and quickly changed into street clothes. He knew time was running out, but he'd had to find a place to clean up and prepare for his next assault on Lenzini's terror network, and this had proved as good a place as any. Still, Bolan wasn't about to count on its security, so he'd left the lights off and navigated by either the night-lights or a small high-powered flashlight. By now, word would be out to the syndicate and its various Families that something bad had gone down in a mob-held operation, and that was going to get people moving. Bolan didn't have any reason to think that he'd be safe behind any doorway the mob darkened.

He withdrew the Desert Eagle and Beretta from their respective holsters, keeping one weapon loaded and at the ready while he quickly stripped and cleaned the other. The Beretta was first. Bolan used a high-pressure spray can of fast-drying, chlorinated solvent that cleared burnt powder residue and fouling from the major assemblies, safety, receiver and barrel of the pistol. He lightly oiled the moving parts and within minutes the Beretta was reassembled and locked and loaded. The warrior repeated these steps for the Desert Eagle, and loaded the .44 Magnum hand cannon before tucking it away in his weapons bag.

Bolan tallied the count of C-4 blocks remaining—it would hardly be enough to bring down any sort of major structure. And since the Executioner wasn't sure what he'd be up against in Seattle, it seemed obvious he was going to need support. He knew just where to get it. At first, he'd considered having Jack Grimaldi fly out and meet him in Seattle, but taking his rental that far would easily mean a drive of twenty-three hours, best speed, and it didn't make sense when the Stony Man flier could be here in four to five. Considering refueling and other variables, that would easily put Bolan in Seattle within twelve hours. That seemed like the best plan. The only thing he would have to do is keep his head down while he waited.

Bolan retrieved the special cellular phone he was carrying. The compact device wasn't much larger than a credit card, and was nearly as thin, but it operated on high-speed alternating frequencies at a rate of seventeen channels per second, thereby making any conversation virtually undetectable. Additionally, it used a satellite communications system devised by Kurtzman and his cybernetics team. Affectionately termed the "Bear phone," the device had almost unlimited range and could pinpoint the position of its user within an error margin of less than a quarter mile, and no error with a satellite visual confirmation.

"It's Striker," Bolan announced to Aaron Kurtzman.

"How's it going?"

"Still on schedule, but I'm running out of time. How are things there?"

"Well, we've got someone at MacEwan's apartment helping to coordinate activities. I've got two of my team working full-time on reverse compiling the code as MacEwan cracks it, and they're writing corresponding assembly language programs to counteract the effects if this thing actually goes live."

"Have you gotten any leads on Rhatib?"

"Nada," Kurtzman replied. "And you should also know that Leo got some buzz on Lenzini's people."

"Let me guess," Bolan interjected. "They're coming for me."

"In numbers, from what I understand."

"Significant?"

"Nothing I'm sure you can't handle," Kurtzman replied. He added, "Unless they get the drop on you first."

Bolan could hear the almost teasing tone in Kurtzman's

voice, and he smiled. There was no question the news was serious, but Bear—in his own unique way—was trying to find a way to make things a bit lighter. That was something they could always count on; Kurtzman's sense of humor held up even when the chips were down. It didn't make the situation any less serious, or the matters any less grave, but it did manage to ignite a small spark of rejuvenation for the men and women of Stony Man who lived in an otherwise grim and bloody world.

It also reminded Mack Bolan that the job he did kept hope alive in that world.

"I'll be watchful," the warrior promised Kurtzman. "In the meantime, I need Eagle out here pronto."

"He's just returned from the infirmary. He was going to pick up Able Team in Texas. Hal turned security of MacEwan's mother over to the U.S. Marshal Service, since she's no longer being watched. We don't have any reason to suspect that members of the NIF will target her, and Hal doesn't think they even know MacEwan's helping us."

"That's fine. How Hal handles that is entirely up to him," Bolan replied. "If Able agrees to defer, how soon do you think Eagle can be here?"

"Not sure of actual flying time, but if he knows you'll need him, I'm sure he'll be out of here within the hour."

"Good enough," Bolan replied. "Tell him I'll need plenty of supplies."

"Anything you need in specific quantities?"

"High-yield explosives, as compact as Cowboy can get them," Bolan replied.

Kurtzman let out a booming chuckle. "Oh, he'll love hearing that. He's got some new stuff he just put together, and he says it will blow your socks off. No pun intended."

"I'm sure if that's what Cowboy said, the pun was very much intended," Bolan said with light laugh.

Bolan suddenly sensed a problem, the hair on the back of his neck standing on end. Something just wasn't right. A car had gone by, and a minute later another car had gone by in the opposite direction, and again a car had passed in the same direction as the first, and at about the same interval. It was too regular to be random traffic, not to mention it seemed suddenly busy at that early-morning hour. And even given the tourism in the area, and the regulars on the beach, Bolan hadn't noticed it was *that* busy. Such activity meant one of two things: cops or bulls.

Mack Bolan was betting it was the latter.

The Executioner moved to the window and carefully parted one of the paper-thin, sheer curtains. A luxury SUV with darkened windows was slowing and pulling to the curb across the street, its lights extinguished.

"Listen, Bear," Bolan said, interrupting whatever Kurtzman had been saying. "I think that trouble you were talking about just showed up. Let Eagle know I'll contact him."

"Understood, Striker, and you be—"

"Out here," Bolan cut in and hung up the phone.

The Executioner watched at the window a moment longer—long enough to see the doors start to open and a group of very tough customers emerge—before packing up his weapons bag.

If at all possible, he was going to exit quietly and avoid any possible confrontation. While the denizens of this building didn't exactly fall into the upstanding citizens category, they were still innocents in this war, and Bolan didn't want to chance being responsible for their deaths.

After locking Pescia's apartment door and heading for the back stairs, an elderly black woman suddenly opened her door and reached down for the newspaper. She stopped when she saw Bolan's shoes, and her eyes trailed up his tall, muscular body to look him square in the eye.

"Who are you?" she asked. "I ain't seen you 'round here before."

Bolan raised his hand and showed her a wan smile. "Nobody important, ma'am. Just go back inside your apartment and don't worry."

The woman placed one hand on her hip, shook the paper at him, and said, "Don't you be giving me no lip, young man. I don't know who you think you are, but you can't talk to me that way. You don't own this place!"

Bolan started for the stairs, figuring that was his signal to just keep going, but the woman seemed intent on following him and scolding him. "Don't you dare walk away from me while I'm talking to you! Didn't your momma ever teach you any manners? You white folk just march in and out of here like you own the place, and—"

The Executioner heard another door open and a louder, male voice cut her off. "Shit, Granny! What you yelling about now?"

Bolan turned and saw a younger man, maybe a teenager or perhaps in his twenties, standing outside his door in boxer shorts and a T-shirt. The old woman didn't say anything, but instead just pointed at Bolan and studied the new arrival expectantly. The young man turned and looked at the Executioner for a moment, their eyes locking, and then he started walking toward Bolan.

"What's happening here, man?" the kid said. "You hassling this woman or something? This is my adopted grandma, whitey. You should be more careful about your business."

Bolan heard the first of the footfalls on the steps, and they were coming pretty quickly. What he didn't have time for was an encounter with the approaching group, and he also didn't want either of Pescia's neigbours to get killed. So the warrior did the only thing he could, reaching inside his jacket and bringing the Beretta into plain view.

"Get yourself and her back inside, and do it *now*," he said.

The kid stopped suddenly, nodded with obvious fear and then turned and tried to hustle the woman into her apartment. She went, but not quietly, and the disturbance had eaten away at the Executioner's window of opportunity. Bolan was ready to make his exit when the men from the SUV appeared at the top of the front stairwell. The soldier immediately recognized the faces of Serge Grano and his lieutenant, Ape. Grano shouted as soon as he saw Bolan, but that was the least of the Executioner's concerns. The young man had managed to get the old woman inside, but he turned to see the Mafia hard guys and he was obviously not content to let this business go. He started toward them, and Bolan knew at that point he had a choice to either escape or save the youth from himself and what was sure to be a swift and violent death. The Executioner realized, even as he ascended the three steps in a single leap and charged the kid from behind, that he'd never really had a choice.

Grano brought out his pistol, but Bolan still had the Beretta in hand. The Executioner snap-aimed and squeezed the trigger twice as he threw his body on top of the kid and sent both of them to the floor. The first shot was high and wide, but the second found flesh. The bullet struck Grano in the shoulder and flipped him off his feet. Two men behind him caught his body, and Ape now had pistol in hand and was ascending the steps in order to get a clear shot. Bolan took a deep breath and squeezed the trigger twice more, this time more sure of his target. Both rounds caught Ape in the face, the first ripping away the upper part of his neck while the second punched through his upper lip and split open the back of his skull. Blood sprayed the wall to his right and his body staggered drunkenly before crashing into Pescia's apartment door and collapsing.

Bolan was on his feet in seconds, and he hauled the kid

with him. He shoved the youth toward the old woman's still partially open apartment door. She stood just inside, screaming with her hands covering her ears. Bolan got the youth through it before closing the door tightly. He assessed his targets before moving the selector switch to 3-shot bursts. The two who had caught Grano were still tending to their wounded boss, while another had produced a .45-caliber pistol and was lining up on Bolan. The Executioner dropped to one knee as the guy opened fire, and two rounds chipped chunks of wood and plaster from the wall.

The Executioner raised the Beretta and squeezed the trigger. This time, three rounds left the muzzle and all three connected with the Mafia gunner's upper torso, catching him in the lower gut, solar plexus and sternum. The man's body jerked spasmodically as blood and pink frothy sputum spewed from his mouth. He fell prone on the steps, his gun flying from deadened fingers, and Bolan could hear the dull thud of the impact even as he turned and descended the stairs.

For a moment, Bolan had been tempted to seize the advantage and take out the remainder of the force, but he could not bring himself to shoot men tending to one of their own wounded. While this was a war of attrition, and not governed by the true conventions of humane warfare—if there could even be such a thing—Bolan found himself compelled to follow certain moral and ethical standards in fighting the enemy. Killing those who were trying to help a wounded comrade went beyond those ethics, and the Executioner wouldn't compromise them. Hell, he *couldn't* compromise them. Otherwise, he became that which he most despised: a barbaric and thoughtless murderer who did not kill for duty or purpose, but instead for lust of blood.

Bolan had reached the first-floor landing and was about to pull the door open when he felt a presence behind him. The Executioner crouched and launched a vicious foot sweep to knock the charging opponent off his feet. At least, Bolan thought that would happen. Instead, the beefy Mafia hood was simply knocked off balance, and the Executioner stepped in to finish the job quickly. Bolan launched a front kick that the guy blocked, not without effort. The man counterattacked with a ham-sized fist to the jaw that sent the warrior reeling into the opposite wall.

The man was big and his punches were like sledgehammers. Bolan could feel it all, the shock to his jaw and the ringing in his ears, but he recovered quickly enough to keep the hulking brute from locking viselike fingers around his throat. Bolan turned into the charge and dropped low, firing an uppercut that had his entire shoulder and right arm in it. His opponent's teeth slammed shut and his head snapped back, but it still wasn't enough to drop the guy. Bolan didn't let up, and he launched an elbow strike to the chest. The blow knocked the wind from the man and cracked bone.

Despite the effect of Bolan's strike, the guy managed to grab the Executioner's hair and land an iron hard punch to his stomach. Bolan felt the wind rush from his lungs in response to the blow, and before he could recover the guy had one hand on his throat. Bolan felt as if his voice box and trachea were about to become mashed together. The Executioner managed to turn enough to loosen the mammoth's grip, and then as he raised his foot to stomp on the guy's instep, he grabbed the handle of the Colt Combat Commander knife he kept strapped to his boot. Bolan let his foot fall on the guy's instep. The man grunted with pain but he didn't loosen his grip at all.

A moment elapsed before the Executioner found the position he needed.

Bolan slashed the back of the guy's hand with the knife, and suddenly he was free. The warrior finished the job quickly, twisting inward and shoving his shoulder against his larger opponent to knock the man off balance. The technique distracted the guy long enough for Bolan to find a new position and in that second of vulnerability, the victor was decided. The Executioner swung upward with the knife blade, driving the point through the guy's throat and burying it to the hilt. The man staggered backward, both hands rushing to pull the knife from the tender tissue as he managed to gurgle a squeal of shock and pain. Only seconds passed before his eyes glazed over, and he collapsed against the wall and slid to the ground.

Bolan put his foot to the guy's chest and removed the bloody knife. He wiped it clean on the dead man's shirt and returned it to its sheath. He quickly retrieved his bag, which he'd dropped during the scuffle and continued to the rear exit door and out into an alley. He couldn't risk going back for his car. He'd grab a cab and head for the airport. That would be a safe enough port at which to wait.

And it would be good to see a familiar face.

16

Washington, D.C.

"You must not go, Malcolm," Sadiq Rhatib said.

"But you see, my dear Sadiq, that is just the point," Malcolm Shurish replied. "I *must* go, for my own sake and for the sake of our mission. If you should fail here—"

"But I won't fail," Rhatib said in protest.

"But if you should, we must be able to implement an alternative strategy, and we must be able to do so quickly. And I am the most logical choice."

Rhatib sighed, and Shurish could tell that he didn't want to give in. Nonetheless, Shurish knew this was their only choice in insuring success, and he was quite aware that Rhatib knew it as well. A disaster was about to unfold, and too many of their previous contingencies were riding on Abdalrahman's success in bringing down the American agent, Cooper. Still, that wasn't enough upon which to bank their entire scheme. Shurish had a "plan B" ready and waiting.

"Do you know where she's being kept?" Rhatib asked.

"Not precisely, but I know that she is back in Washington, and I know she's helping them try to shut down our system," Shurish replied. "I've been tracking her little steps. She is so predictable that I cannot help but laugh. Who else has such a unique signature? The woman has no concept of security.

She's leaves a trail of clues to her identity wherever she goes. She has no idea that my program can instantly detect anyone who attempts to crack the security codes I've put in place."

"Not to mention that you predicted *exactly* what they would look for in this network of Lenzini's." Rhatib smiled and added, "My uncle was not entirely fair with you, Malcolm. You are truly brilliant in some ways. In fact, your genius very much mirrors my own."

"It is kind of you to say so," Shurish replied with a bow, although he wasn't really feeling that kind of respect.

There was no mistaking the fact that Sadiq Rhatib was exceptionally brilliant. Shurish would have been the first to admit it. But Rhatib's genius had been limited. His intellectual maturity had been stunted by Abdalrahman, who had brainwashed him with high ideals of religion and duty to country. Nonetheless, Rhatib *had* managed to penetrate the Carnivore system for a short time, and he'd also cooked up the idea of enlisting American companies to unwittingly aid in their cause. It was the greed and capitalism of the West that caused them to be so short-sighted when it came to battling against terrorists.

"Still, I would not underestimate her, or the resolve of her friends," Rhatib continued. "You recall that she proved herself quite competent, and was even able to ruin my plans to turn American society on its ear using Carnivore. It was her accursed interference that set back my original timetable and nearly ruined our plans."

"Patience, my young friend," Shurish replied. The statement was genuine, although he heard the mocking in own tone of voice. "You are beginning to sound like your uncle. We will deal with this woman, but in our own good time. The most important thing is for us to concentrate on completing the plan. Once the network is in place and locked down, and I've activated the code, we will not only have control of the majority of American defense systems, but we will also control the better part of the Internet.

"And then we shall use those defenses to destroy the military capabilities of other countries. We shall use American missiles to defeat aircraft, American bombs to level cities. And then, when we have banded the other countries in support of Islam behind us, we will launch our own attack and simply shut down their defenses," Shurish said proudly.

Rhatib clapped his hands together and gleefully interjected, "We will bring this country to its knees!"

"Imagine it," Shurish said, looking off into the distance, his mind racing with the thrill of their plans. "Imagine the look of shock on the Americans' faces when their systems suddenly shoot down British and Israeli planes. Imagine how puzzled they'll be if they are subjected to attacks and, despite all of their efforts, they are unable to respond."

"Military stockpiles will dwindle quickly as well," Rhatib declared. "And as the Americans lose faith in the ability of their government to stop the nightmare, trading will stagnate, and this capitalist and imperialist economy on which they have so long relied will collapse under their feet! Corporations will lose billions of dollars, because stock trading and buying and selling will be in our control! Millions of dollars will disappear with the push of a button!"

"And they'll be powerless to stop any of it!" Shurish could hardly hold back the emotions that swept over him. The scientist willed himself to become calm. Of course, it wasn't over yet, and there was always a chance of failure as long as Cooper and MacEwan still drew a breath. He would have to instigate his alternate plan quickly, if all was to go as he'd designed it.

"I must leave you now, my friend," he said, grabbing Rhatib by the shoulders and embracing him ceremonially.

"May Allah guide your steps, Malcolm," Rhatib said.

"And yours, my brother."

Shurish left the makeshift complex and drove toward Washington, D.C. He watched carefully to insure he wasn't being followed. It was true that he trusted Sadiq much more than he would ever trust Abdalrahman, but he felt like things were beginning to unravel. He had to be ready with an alternate plan—and he had one—and to use every strategy to protect himself if Abdalrahman was unsuccessful in his mission to destroy Cooper.

Very few people knew that Shurish had masterminded this entire thing. He'd pulled all of the strings, made the arrangements and even gotten the NIF operating inside American borders virtually undetected. He had forged the alliance with Nicolas Lenzini and had arranged for the networking of Lenzini's systems to American defense computers. But most importantly, he was the one who had engineered and devised the plan to use Rhatib's technical genius to hack into the Carnivore system and divert attention way from the real plan.

The very thought of it made him smile.

Despite what Umar or Sadiq thought, it was Shurish who had real control over the system. The military leaders at the Pentagon and fellow scientists at DARPA had laughed at him when he first proposed Operation Poltergeist. It was too costly, some had said, while others presumed it simply wasn't worth the effort to investigate further. That had been the final straw for Shurish. Malcolm Shurish, Ph.D. in information systems with a concentration in artificial intelligence, and he wasn't good enough for his own country. That was right after the attacks on the World Trade Center, and that was when he'd decided America had gotten exactly what it deserved. He was one of them, but they treated him like a criminal. They interrogated him and questioned his ethics and practices; they searched his home and grilled his relatives; they temporarily suspended him from any sensitive projects and it was some time before he was fully reinstated.

All of that after what he'd done for what he'd thought were his government and his people. In one sense, Umar was correct that they were no longer his people. Still, he could not help but feel some devotion and allegiance to them. He didn't want to destroy them, but he was dismayed by the smug arrogance with which the country's military leaders had treated him. He had an IQ that well exceeded the limits of anything those small-minded generals could ever hope to achieve, and he didn't feel he should have to prove that genius.

In fact, it was time for him to use some of that genius now. He removed his cell phone from the console where it had been charging and dialed a special access number into DARPA headquarters. An operator answered immediately.

"Yes, this is Dr. Shurish," he said. "My code clearance authorization is one-seven-two-nine-five-alpha-gamma-delta, code word for this period is periwinkle."

"One moment, sir, while we confirm your authorization and code," the operator dutifully replied.

Shurish could hear her typing the information into their computer systems. The very thought was almost laughable, since he was basically in control of those systems. With the aid of other scientists, he'd designed them and he knew every back door and security hole in them. But the operator could go on and verify all that she wanted to verify—he had all the time in the world.

"Your authorization is clear, Dr. Shurish," the operator replied. "What is your request?"

"I need to place an emergency call to Tyra MacEwan," he said calmly. He gave the operator the number to the specially encrypted cellular phone she would be carrying.

Shurish was confident she would have the phone with her. Employees of the Defense Advance Research Projects Agency were required to carry it everywhere, even off duty, and old habits died hard. Even if she was under the protection of a secret federal agency—which was obviously the same agency that Cooper worked for—she would have insisted on keeping it with her. MacEwan was all about duty and country and honor; he knew because he'd once been just like her—an eager, wide-eyed youth trying to move up in the system, and struggling hard for years before he finally became deputy director of the Information Processing and Technology Office. In fact, he was now acting director since his boss had gone on a ski vacation in the Alps with his family. Tragically no one had heard from him in months, nor his wife and children. It was just another example of Shurish's ingenuity, and his ability to remove anyone who stood in his path.

The familiar, husky voice came on the line and broke Shurish from his reverie. "This is MacEwan."

"Tyra, this is Dr. Shurish."

"Malcolm?" There was a long pause, and Shurish could tell immediately someone was with her. He heard furious typing at the keyboard, but only a moment elapsed before her voice filled his ear again. "Where are you? Do you realize they're looking everywhere for you?"

"Who is looking for me, Tyra?" Shurish asked.

"Well, um, the FBI for starters!" she exclaimed.

Shurish could hardly contain his laughter, thinking about how quickly she'd had to recover from *that* one.

"Our own people are searching for you, as well. They say you've done something wrong, Malcolm. They're telling me that you orchestrated this whole thing."

"I have done no such thing, Tyra," Shurish said, trying his best to sound frightened. "You *must* believe me. I've been hiding for days, practically since you got back. There are these men…"

"What men, Malcolm?" MacEwan asked. *"What men?"*

"I don't know who they are, but they're definitely terrorists," he said. "I'm sure of it! Tyra, I must meet with you.

There's nobody else I can trust, and I know if you just hear me out, if you just hear what I have to say, that you'll believe me. I've never given you any reason to doubt me."

"I don't know, Malcolm," MacEwan replied. "I don't know if they would allow me to go. I'm sure I'm being watched."

"You *must* meet me, Tyra!"

"You should turn yourself in," she said quietly.

"I can't!" he exclaimed, pouring it on thickly now. "They'll come for me. The government can't protect me. Look at what happened to you. They could barely protect *you!*"

"But they have protected me, Malcolm," MacEwan insisted.

Shurish was beginning to wonder if this was going to be as easy as he'd first envisioned. They were definitely trying to use technical methods, probably by hacking into DARPA computers, to track his signal. Not that it mattered—Shurish had already thought of that. The system was currently bouncing the signal all over Washington, thereby making any sort of true triangulation of his position impossible. Not to mention the fact that he'd removed the global positioning satellite chip from the receiver long ago, and replaced it with a ghosting device. If they attempted a satellite downlink to the phone, all it would do was echo a return signal that amounted to little more than high-frequency gibberish.

"Don't try to track me, Tyra," Shurish told her. Maybe if he was honest, he could convince her that he was innocent of any wrongdoing. "I *swear* to you that I've done nothing wrong."

"What about Poltergeist, Malcolm?" MacEwan asked. "Did you think I wouldn't remember your Poltergeist program?"

"They stole it from me," Shurish replied. "Don't you see?

They set me up at the very beginning to take the fall, and I let them do it. Don't you remember everything they put me through? Have you forgotten so soon, Tyra? They tried to find wrongdoing in everything I was and everything I created, but I came up innocent. I came up clean, just I am clean now. Please, you have to help me. Please, Tyra… Please…"

And then he began to sob, softly and gently, but just enough to make her believe he was desperate for her help. She was a soft touch—he knew that about her—and it was this weakness he would play on. MacEwan was always ready to help the underdog; she always wanted to do the right thing, and this was her chance. She would see this as an opportunity to right a wrong and redeem a friend.

"All right," she whispered. "Tell me where and when."

Tyra MacEwan could hardly believe she'd agreed to do it.

She knew what she should have done was to contact Cooper's people, or told the people guarding her, but she wasn't sure how fair they would be with Shurish. She couldn't very well tell the FBI or the U.S. Marshals, since they were both working for whoever was pulling the government strings here. Then again, she didn't believe this was some conspiracy, either. All she could do was hear him out, and that's exactly what she intended to do.

First, she left the guy they had assigned to help her sitting at the systems with some labor-intensive assignment that would keep him busy the rest of the morning and probably well into the day. With that part taken care of, she then told him she was going to take a shower and get some rest. She went into the master bedroom, locked the door and then turned on the shower. There was a window that led onto a fire escape, and after donning warm clothes and a jacket—careful to insure she brought her wallet and phone—MacEwan went out the window and down the ladder until she reached the alleyway below.

Much to her dismay, MacEwan realized there was no exit

to the rear. That meant she'd have to find some way of getting past the guards posted in a vehicle parked outside the apartment building. That was no mean trick, and since she couldn't scale the side of the adjoining brick building, or leap the gaps between the two roofs without breaking every bone in her body, her ability to escape would be solely determined by how clever she could actually be. It didn't take her long to come up with a plan, and a highway billboard—visible from the alley—gave her the idea. It was a picture of a fireman holding a young child, both of them covered in soot and ash, and a caption cautioning children not to play with matches.

MacEwan dialed the fire department immediately. She didn't want to send them out on an emergency run, just in case they would be needed somewhere else, so she asked for assistance from them in lighting her furnace. That would be considered a public assistance call, and it would be the lowest priority—thus it wouldn't divert them if a true emergency came in. Still, it was going to cause quite a ruckus, since she'd called it for the old woman she noticed living in the apartment below. True to form, the fire department, an engine led by an officer's car, showed up within ten minutes—ready to render whatever assistance they could—and pulled up right in front of the building. With all due diligence, the firefighters climbed from the truck and went inside. MacEwan peered out of the alleyway and saw that truck was completely blocking the view of the agents. She burst from concealment and headed to the next corner. Fortunately, as throughout much of D.C., there were a line of cabs waiting on the busy side street.

MacEwan climbed into the first cab and gave the driver the address. Actually, it surprised her that Malcolm had wanted to meet in the parking lot of the DARPA offices. That didn't seem quite right for a man fearful for his own life, and moreover a man who was trying to escape detection. Nonetheless, she wasn't going to question it. She'd known Malcolm Shurish for years, and she'd never known him to be deceitful. He'd always been wholly dedicated to his work, and she had no reason to believe he'd lie to her now. Besides, it didn't hurt to listen. And she wasn't afraid he'd do anything, because if this was all just a deception, she had her gun and she was quite able to protect herself.

What made her feel guilty was leaving Cooper and his friends in the lurch. She wasn't holding up her end of the bargain, but from what she understood recently, her mother was no longer in danger. So really, the terms of the deal were off. Nonetheless, she was a woman of her word, and she would complete her assignment. But she couldn't do that effectively if Shurish was being wrongly targeted, and the real terrorists were still out there and plotting America's destruction. And if Shurish *was* innocent of any wrongdoing, then he would be willing to come back with her and help her crack the code. That would prove his innocence and show the government, once and for all, that he was a patriot and ready to do whatever was necessary to protect his country.

MacEwan arrived at the DARPA offices. The parking lot was deserted, save for a few cars, and she wondered how silly it would look for her to show up in a cab and then just stand outside waiting. Fortunately, she didn't have to wait, because as soon as she'd paid the cabbie and he was out of sight, Shurish pulled up in his car. MacEwan got in immediately and soon the two were on their way, headed down the interstate and out of Washington.

"Where are we going?" MacEwan asked.

"To my house," Shurish told her.

"Won't they be watching for you there?"

"I don't think so," he said. "They've already been there and searched the place. I sincerely doubt they will return."

"Malcolm, you *must* tell me what's going on. I've risked my neck to get to you, and I think you owe me an explanation."

"Soon, my dear," he replied. "Very soon I will explain it all."

"No, Malcolm, you will explain it now."

He moved so quickly that MacEwan didn't have time to react. She hadn't known he was capable of such speed, otherwise she would have better prepared herself. She felt something small and sharp strike her in the side of the neck, something he was holding in his hand, but when she tried to reach for the pistol in the pocket of her overcoat, she was unable to move. It was almost as if something had paralyzed her. And then she could hear him laughing and talking, but she couldn't really understand what he was saying.

The world closed in around her, and all she saw was darkness....

17

Seattle, Washington

"Disappeared?" Bolan said, echoing Brognola's words. "What do you mean disappeared? People don't just vanish into thin air, Hal."

"All other things being equal," Brognola replied, "I'd agree with you, Striker. But this is a special circumstance."

The Executioner was safely aboard a Learjet C-21A, his trusted friend and pilot at the stick. Jack Grimaldi had been through many of the same hells Bolan had, most at a higher elevation, but he was a tough SOB and a hard-charger all the same. The Executioner respected him, not just for his guts and his spirit, but also for his undivided loyalty and unswerving devotion to their friendship. Not to mention the fact the guy was one of the best damn pilots on the planet—no, *the* best— and Bolan could always count on him to be there when he was most needed.

"She did it on her own," Bolan continued. "Didn't she?"

"We think so, yes. Unless somebody snatched her out of the shower and carried her down the fire escape. But I'm not real sure I'm buying that since you'd think someone would notice a wet, naked woman being carried down the sidewalk during morning rush hour."

"So what's your next move?" Bolan asked.

"Well, we believe that if she left it was probably to meet someone. The guy we sent to work with her was positive that he heard her talking to someone. We had the phones bugged, and nothing came in on that. She must have had her own phone. We also talked with her mother, and she swears that MacEwan never called her, or vice versa."

"So she just got up and walked out."

"Well, it's possible she set up a decoy. About thirty minutes before our guy decided to check on her, and subsequently discovered she was missing, a fire truck arrived for what they say was a public assistance call to light the furnace of the woman downstairs."

"Okay, so we think she used that as a diversion."

"Yes, and it would have been a pretty clever one except for the fact that the entire building is heated by a single boiler in the basement. There's no furnace to light, and there are no individual heating units in the apartments. We make sure that thing undergoes regular maintenance, seeing as it's one of our safehouses."

"And to prevent someone from doing exactly what she did."

"Precisely," Brognola replied, "although the fire department didn't have any way of knowing that at the time. We'd always counted on any deceptions of that nature to come through the nine-one-one system. I don't think anybody would have accounted for a call from the operator direct to one of the station houses."

"Like I told you before, she's one sharp cookie."

"Well, since we know she didn't get a call over that number and she wasn't talking to her mother, we're guessing she set up the whole thing so she could slip away. That leaves us believing she did it so she could meet someone."

It only took Bolan a second to come up with a name. "Shurish."

"That's what we're thinking, as well."

"That guy is slippery, Hal. You need to find him, and you need to find him quick, or I guarantee you that's the last we'll see of MacEwan."

"I've got Able Team on its way back right now," he replied. "The guys will start scouring the city and work their way out. In the meantime, I assume you're still going after your final target."

"Well, at least the final target out here. The last target is in Boston."

"You're talking about Lenzini?"

"Yeah."

"Actually, he's here in Washington according to all of the intelligence we've had in the past twenty-four hours. And, we suspect that the NIF may finally be on to you. The little numbers you did on the Mob in San Francisco and Los Angeles have effectively neutralized their operations. Lenzini's seething, and the phone taps we have say he's no longer willing to commit resources."

"Wait until talk of my latest exploits gets back to him," Bolan grumbled. "He's out one lieutenant, and I don't think that Serge Grano's going to be in any shape to come after me for a while. By the time he's ready to take up the sword again, his boss will be long dead."

"Well, watch for the NIF, Striker. We've got intelligence briefings on some very strange movements. We now believe that Umar Abdalrahman's in this country, and we think he's coming after you. He might even try to stop you before you reach Seattle."

"I'll be watching for him. And, Hal?"

"Yes?"

"Find MacEwan," Bolan said quietly. "Find her before it's too late for all of us."

"We'll do everything we can, Striker. Good luck."

"Out here."

Bolan signed off and switched back to the plane's internal frequency. For a while, he just looked out the window at the twinkling lights twenty-thousand feet below. Every so often, the lights would disappear and the plane's flashing strobes would reflect off a thick, billowing cover of clouds. Sometimes, the cloud cover wasn't so thick, and then it was like floating through a translucent sheet of cotton. The Executioner was avoiding an uncomfortable conversation with Grimaldi regarding Tyra MacEwan's disappearance. He knew Grimaldi heard every word that had been said.

The Executioner fixed his friend with a concerned stare. "You feeling all right, Jack?"

"Still a bit sore from the number they did on me in Afghanistan," Grimaldi replied. "But I'm hanging in there, Sarge. How about you? Are you doing okay?"

"What do you mean?"

"Well, I know you're only asking me if I'm feeling all right because of the fact MacEwan ran off to who knows where."

"Yeah, well, maybe a little, Jack."

"Listen, Sarge, there isn't a damn thing anybody can do about it. MacEwan knew the risks and she also knew what could happen if she left the protection umbrella. I'm sure she was just doing whatever she thought was right, and I'm also sure she's smart enough to take care of herself."

"Yeah, I guess you're thinking straight on this."

Grimaldi fired the Executioner a wicked grin and a wink, and then said, "Of course I am. Just lie down on the couch back there and we'll talk about anything else you'd like."

"All right," Bolan said, raising his hands in mock surrender. "I get the point."

"What's your plan?"

"I figured it's time for us to dish out some of what we took in Afghanistan," Bolan replied. "So if you're looking for some payback, now would be the time. Feel like some action?"

"Depends," Grimaldi replied. "I'd prefer an F-18 Hornet, but this'll do for us. She's been modified with the usual compliment of four 30 mm cannons, and the underside is equipped with a pair of AGM-130s."

The Executioner nodded, quite impressed with the modifications to the civilian Learjet. Just one of AGM-130s would do well against the major network hub rumored to be outside of Seattle. The AGM was a guided, air-to-surface missile, and could be fired and targeted by Grimaldi from the cockpit. The missile was commonly deployed by the Air Force, and its weapons systems officers swore it was perfect for taking out preplanned targets as well as targets of opportunity. It would be more than enough to handle anything the NIF could throw at them.

"You'll be able to trigger this thing once it hits?" Bolan asked.

"Roger that," Stony Man's ace flier replied. "Those babies can go off either on impact or by triggering. I can make sure it's well into the ground before I let her go."

"Good, because I'd hate to have civilian casualties out of this. All right, here's the plan then. It should be dark by the time we get over the target. I'll do a high-level jump first, and that should give you time to touch down and fuel. I want to make sure we're clear of bystanders before you do your stuff. Once we're clear of this, I'll head for the airport and meet up with you there."

"Sounds like a plan," Grimaldi replied. "You just make sure you're out there before I come in, Sarge. I'd hate to see you get fried crisp with the bad guys."

Bolan nodded. Turning high-yield military payloads out on civilian areas wasn't exactly his first choice, but there was a lot more at stake if they didn't accomplish the mission. Truthfully, the Executioner didn't have any idea what he'd be up against. The entire thing was difficult to predict. One thing he *did* know was that his country was counting on him. If he didn't stop it here and now, the terrorists stood a big chance of seeing their plans come to fruition, and who knew what would happen then. Just as before, he didn't have any choice. There was no way in hell he could let them get away with it.

No way in hell. Yeah.

THE JUMP STARTED just like any other, although Bolan couldn't remember the last time he'd had to parachute into a location in his own country.

Well, the ends would justify the means. Bolan clicked on his radio as soon as his chute had fully deployed, and tested his signal to Grimaldi. The pilot came back in a crackled but clear enough reply. Bolan figured he'd have thirty-seven minutes tops, provided everything went on schedule, and that was a best guess since he didn't really have a schedule. He landed without incident, and five precious minutes elapsed while he disconnected his chute and cleared himself from his jumping gear. Add to that the three minutes from jump point to ground, and he was down to under thirty to accomplish his mission.

Fortunately, his parachute had provided significant guidance and given the low winds, he was on target. The bright lights surrounding the perimeter of the huge warehouse complex were visible in the distance. Bolan began to trot through the deep, marshy grasses. He ignored the cold splashes of water that doused his boots and the pants of the clean blacksuit Grimaldi had brought. He'd managed a few hours of sleep during the flight and had eaten a hot MRE.

The Executioner wasn't the only one rejuvenated. Strapped beneath his left arm was the well-oiled, fully loaded Beretta 93-R with two spare magazines, and the Desert Eagle riding in a low-slung holster on his right thigh. He wasn't carrying grenades or wearing a harness, but there were spare 30-round magazines tucked into concealed pockets of the blacksuit for the M-16 A-2 clutched in his fists. The warrior was prepared for combat, and he was planning on bringing his own unique brand of justice to the enemy.

At a nice, even pace to reduce the risk of injury from a sprained ankle or a fall, Bolan managed to reach the warehouse complex in twenty minutes. He went prone at a corner post of the ten-foot-high fence that lined the perimeter, careful to remain in the shadows. The place didn't look like it was heavily guarded, but the Executioner quickly changed his mind when he saw a white pickup truck driving along the perimeter. Besides a driver, an orange light flashing atop the cab illuminated two men seated on the back rails of the pickup, each carrying some sort of hardware. They looked like bolt-action rifles, but Bolan couldn't be absolutely sure from that distance; he would assume the worst until some other hard evidence presented itself.

The soldier turned an upward glance to three towers of various heights, the tallest looked like a miniature water tower, and stood as high as the main warehouse. The other two were clearly observation towers, lower in height, but Bolan couldn't see anyone manning them at the moment. It was possible the two in back of the pickup truck were simply hitching a ride, and that was exactly where they were headed.

In that case, Bolan would have to make sure they never reached their destination. The Executioner did another scan of the area and then went to one knee and removed a pair of heavy-duty wire cutters from the hollowed butt of the M-16 A-2, normally reserved for a cleaning kit. The Executioner tapped the wire cutters against the fence rapidly to insure it wasn't electrified, and then went about the work of gaining entry. Once he'd created a large enough egress, he pushed his way inside, stored the wire cutters and did another assessment. He couldn't see the truck any longer, and that concerned him. He didn't know much about the place. For all his intelligence—none—it could have been equipped with a full alarm system or a division of NIF troops posing as security.

One thing Bolan did know was the security guards weren't typical security officers. This place was supposed to be a toy manufacturer, and the soldier found it hard to believe that guards with high-powered sniper rifles would need to guard the complex from towers. Or, for that matter, that the place would be lit up like a Christmas tree at this late hour, regardless of whether it was close to the holidays or not. That left nothing but the greatest evidence things weren't as they seemed.

Bolan started to move across the pavement of the lot when the truck suddenly reappeared. It stopped near the tower and a guard was looking toward Bolan. The Executioner dropped to one knee, raised the M-16 A-2 to his shoulder, and sighted down the rail on his target. He moved the selector to single shot, took a breath and let half out, and then squeezed the trigger. The 5.56 mm round left the muzzle of the weapon at 950 meters per second and drilled into the guard before he could take aim himself. The terrorist's body landed in the back of the pickup with a crash.

Bolan had the second guard in sight before the guy even knew what had happened. The look of surprise on his face disappeared when the Executioner took him with a round clean through the chest. Blood spurted from the wound as the man dropped his rifle and toppled out of the back of the pickup.

The driver jumped from the cab, trying to figure out what all of the commotion was about. The Executioner took the shot, catching the terrorist in the spine and throwing his body to the pavement.

Bolan got to his feet and stopped to listen. He waited for alarms, but he didn't hear any. What he did hear were shouts of surprise and accented voices yelling at him. He turned to see a group of five armed terrorists running from a door at the side of the warehouse. It occurred to the Executioner that he might very well have just killed three security guards doing their job, but the men now rushing him and carrying a variety of machine pistols and assault rifles dispelled any such doubts. These men were responding with the training and fervor of fanatical terrorists, and Bolan knew that MO well.

The Executioner wheeled and dashed for the cover of some fifty-five-gallon drums he hoped weren't filled with anything combustible. Still, it was better than getting ventilated by the maelstrom of autofire now directed his way. The muzzles of machine pistols and automatic rifles winked with anger as the terrorists took up a combination of kneeling and standing positions and buzzed the air around him with 9 mm and 7.62 mm slugs.

Bolan took his time, but hammered out his own defense with ferocity and courage. He now moved the selector to 3-round bursts and took his first target in the chest. The burst spun the terrorist gunner, ripping holes in tender flesh and dumping him to pavement. Pools of blood began to form beneath him as Bolan subjected a second terrorist to the same punishment. The air was alive with gunfire now, some of the rounds coming from the terrorists' tracers that crisscrossed the area.

The Executioner changed positions as too many of the rounds were coming close. One ricocheted off the pavement near his boot, a fragment lodging itself in the fleshy portion of his thigh. Bolan bit back the pain and continued returning fire, ignoring the burning in his leg. If he let a scratch like that break his concentration, he'd have much more to worry about—or maybe he'd have nothing to worry about. In either case, he couldn't fail and this wasn't really where he wanted his final showdown to be. Bolan wished he'd brought along some grenades, but he didn't have a hell of a lot of time. What he needed against these kinds of numbers was higher ground.

The Executioner left his lifesaving cover and rushed toward the truck. If he could get up that ladder and into the tower, he stood half a chance against the enemy troops, which now seemed to be appearing exponentially and converging on his position. Bolan slung his weapon as he reached the truck, leaped into the back of the bed and hit the sixth rung of the ladder from there. He scrambled up the ladder, wasting no time at all. He could hear the rounds sizzling past him, and he breathed a sigh of relief as he reached the circular tubing that surrounded the upper part of the ladder that probably served to protect it from rain or ice accumulation.

Bolan reached the top of the tower and looked down in time to see a horde of terrorists approaching. It was now or never, and the Executioner hoped for a payoff. He wasn't disappointed as he unleashed a furious storm of hot lead on the terrorists attempting to gather at the base of the tower. Bolan delivered volley after calculated volley, dropping the terrorists before they could reach the rungs of the ladder. When one or two managed to flank his position and tried to approach from the back side, Bolan would simply trade off positions and take them through the opening in the ladder well.

Finally, after he had decimated a considerable number of the troops, the terrorists decided to forgo their enthusiasm for a more sensible approach, and they started taking covering positions that afforded them a half-decent field of fire but did not allow the Executioner such advantage. One terrorist made a beeline for the opposing tower, but Bolan got him with a 3-round burst before he'd made it two-thirds of the way.

Victory was in his grasp, and he could almost taste it. There was no way they could take him out from this vantage point, unless they started bringing in heavy artillery. The very thought had to have crossed their minds as well, because

Bolan saw two of them emerging and carrying a large tube into position behind some large crates. The Executioner couldn't be positive, but it looked like an Israeli-made 82 mm B-300. The light antiarmor weapon was more than enough to take out a flimsy iron and prefab tower held together by commercial-grade rivets.

The tower suddenly trembled violently. Bolan looked down through the well and watched as the pickup truck suddenly came into view, its tail ramming into the tower base. Bolan grabbed the railing in time to keep himself from being tossed down the ladder. And then he cursed himself for having been so stupid. He'd trapped himself on top of this tower, with half the NIF's forces coming down on him from all directions.

And he didn't have a damn place to go!

18

Between the constant pounding against the base of the tower and the pair working fervently to set up their rocket launcher, Mack Bolan knew he had only a minute to formulate a plan.

The Executioner realized an attempt to descend the ladder would be suicide; the NIF terrorists would fill him with holes before he'd gone five feet. The only option was to find another way out of the tower, and a quick look down and to the right provided the answer. There was a smaller building there, perhaps a boiler room or utility station of some kind, and it looked like a reasonable jump. Bolan judged the distance and did a quick calculation. It was about twenty-eight feet to that rooftop—easily more than four times his height— so he figured there was about a forty-eight percent chance of suffering significant injury.

Still, the soldier considered it a better choice than dying in the collapse of the tower or getting blown to bits while still in it.

Bolan had made his decision, when another idea came to him—he could lessen the risk of injury by decreasing the distance some. It was a risky gamble, but he would have to chance it. And the only way it would work is if he could keep the two terrorists with the rocket launcher busy long enough for the pickup truck to do its work. As if on cue, the tower shuddered under another jarring impact, and Bolan's ears rang as the vibration went through his entire body.

The Executioner quickly removed the sling from his rifle, then passed it through the metal framework bordering the viewing window and lashed it tight with a slipknot. The warrior then wrapped one end around his right fist twice while using his left hand to fire bursts at the terrorists trying to prepare the B-300. Bolan waited until the next jolt from the pickup truck before swinging one leg out of the tower, followed by the other. The warrior hoped the sling would hold his weight. He managed to get both feet onto the ledge of the open viewing window and then shimmied up the tower until reaching its roof.

Rounds whizzed past his head as a few of the troops tried to take advantage of his precarious situation, but at that distance and firing upward, they weren't having a whole lot of luck. Bolan managed to get to the roof and went prone before any of the terrorists could claim their prize. The Executioner switched out clips and sent a few more volleys into the terrorists below. Their muzzles winked with return fire, but Bolan was in such a good position that it would have been almost impossible for them to hit him. He was able to pick them off singly and, in some cases, pairs.

There was a sudden crackle in the headset he wore, and the voice of Jack Grimaldi broke through. "Striker, this is Eagle One. Do you copy?"

"I copy, Eagle One."

"I am up and loaded for bear," Grimaldi replied. "Two minute ETA to your location."

"Striker copies, Eagle One. I'm hot here and having a bit of trouble. Can you give me a low pass and pour on some rain before the big finale?"

"Roger that, Striker. Eagle One is inbound," Grimaldi replied with glee.

Bolan didn't hear anything at first, but that wasn't surprising since Grimaldi would come in low and fast, and be on top of the NIF troops before they knew what had hit them. He had less than two minutes to get down and get out. He'd advised Grimaldi that he was to put the missile into the complex and trigger at the zero hour, regardless of whether he was out of the area. The Executioner knew that Grimaldi would never obey such an order, but there wasn't much Bolan could do about it. If it got to the wire, he knew the Stony Man flier would do whatever was necessary to accomplish the mission—and he'd live with that decision for the rest of his life.

The Executioner could not ask his friend to do that; it had to be Grimaldi's decision and his decision alone.

Bolan was changing out to his last magazine when the sound of the Learjet came from nowhere, and the night sky was suddenly lit with flame and noise. The 30 mm cannons made short work of the area as Grimaldi came in low and hard and poured on the heat.

"Yeeeeee-haw!" Bolan heard through his headset. "Let's rock 'n' roll!"

In the lights of the tracer rounds from the cannons, Bolan could see the surprise on the faces of his enemies. Bodies were ripped apart by the heavy-caliber fire, the military-grade ammunition hitting hard and fast, and tearing away limbs and heads from torsos. Bolan turned to watch the pair with B-300 now trying to acquire this new target, but they stood a very small chance of taking out something with that kind of speed. Had they been deploying a Stinger or other missile of that type, it might have been another story, but in this case the Executioner wasn't too worried. What Grimaldi's maneuver had done was take the heat off of him, and Bolan knew—even as he felt another bone-jarring impact against the tower—that it was time to prepare.

At first, the aftermath of the Learjet passing brought an unsettling quiet to the immediate area, and then there was the sound of creaking metal. Bolan could feel the tower start to sway. Another impact from the pickup truck caused the distressed wood and metal to crumble, and the tower started to fall, headed directly for the rooftop Bolan had spied earlier. The Executioner held on tightly to the sling of the M-16 A-2 and braced both feet against the roof as the tower began to fall. The movement seemed slow and controlled, and Bolan knew his timing would have to be perfect to avoid injury.

The rooftop came toward him fast, but Bolan's resolve remained firm, and at the precise moment he released his hold on the strap and jumped to the rooftop. The Executioner rolled out of the landing to his feet and headed for the edge of the roof. He jumped again, this time coming to the ground as a supporting frame caught the opposite side of the roof, and the smaller building collapsed under its weight. Bolan had barely avoided being crushed under the rubble, and it was only through some miracle he'd never be able to explain that he'd survived the incident unscathed.

Bolan got wearily to his feet and headed for the warehouse.

Grimaldi's voice sounded in his ears. "Eagle One to Striker. You still in the game, Sarge?"

"You bet, Eagle One," Bolan replied. "I'm headed into the warehouse to make sure no innocents are there."

"You want to push out the timeline? You've only got about one-thirty left, Striker."

"Negative, Eagle One, you stay on the original timeline. Do you copy? I'm calling the ball on it, and in one minute, thirty seconds you bring it down."

"Eagle One copies, Striker. But what if you're not out?"

"Then that's checkmate," Bolan replied, and he clicked off his headset.

He hoped those weren't the last words he left with his long-time friend. Grimaldi had accompanied him on many missions, and recently he'd been subjected to some inhumane treatment and outright torture by the hands of their enemies. Still, the ace pilot knew better than anyone that this was why they had to stop the NIF at *any* sacrifice. While a number of the Stony Man warriors would have disagreed, Mack Bolan was as expendable as any of them. He'd chosen to pursue missions on his own, and while he was grateful for the support of the Stony Man crew, he'd kept the alliance tentative so that they wouldn't lose sight of the goal. In Bolan's mind, the minute one of them became more important than victory over animal predators like the NIF, all of their sacrifice, all of the bloodshed and tears and hard work, would be for naught.

And that was simply *not* acceptable.

The Executioner entered the warehouse through a side door and was immediately shocked by the sight. The satellite dish was monstrous, larger than any he had ever seen before, and he now understood why the area was so important to the success of Lenzini's operations and, subsequently, the NIF's ability to control American defense systems. The thing sat on a triangular framework of interconnected metal poles, and stood at least five stories off the ground. The dish itself was rectangular in shape, and it bristled with assemblies of sensory equipment. The satellite dish extended across the entire length of the warehouse, which measured at least one hundred yards or more, and there was a throbbing that seemed to emanate from the very ground on which the device stood.

Bolan couldn't see anyone inside the actual warehouse, which meant that it was probably being controlled by the source system back in Washington. The Executioner started to turn to leave the warehouse when a tall, muscular figure stepped from the shadows, a pistol clutched in its grasp. He had dark, intense eyes and a beard of black streaked with gray, and there was a crazed look in his eyes; it was a look the Executioner had seen a million times before. It emanated with hatred and bloodlust, and the man stared at Bolan with a murderous expression.

"Cooper," the man stated.

"Who are you?" Bolan replied.

"My name is Colonel Umar Abdalrahman," he said. "And it is my destiny to kill you."

"Is that right?"

"I would not take such an insolent tone, Cooper," the terrorist said coldly. "It would appear I have the advantage."

"That's what you think," Bolan replied.

The Executioner whipped his rifle around and tossed it at the man. It wasn't much of a distraction, but it was enough to get Bolan out of the line of fire. A single shot rang out before the warrior tackled Abdalrahman at the knees and slammed his back to the ground. The terrorist recovered quickly, kicking at Bolan and trying to crush his skull with the heel of his boot. Bolan avoided the main thrust of the blow, but the side of the boot scraped against his face. The Executioner willed the pain away as he rolled and got to his feet.

Abdalrahman searched for the gun he'd dropped, but it was no longer in sight. The terrorist reached behind his back and the sound of a knife rasping from a sheath was barely audible. The light playing through the windows from the security lights outside glinted off the large blade. Bolan reached to his boot and withdrew the Colt Combat Commander knife, which practically leaped into his hand as it was released from the spring-loaded sheath.

The two men circled each other, Abdalrahman taking a very odd pose of readiness while the Executioner maintained a low center of gravity, the knife blade held parallel to his forearm with the blade facing away from him. Abdalrahman screamed and charged suddenly, and Bolan easily side-stepped. The terrorist executed a feint of a forward thrust but quickly changed direction as he slid past Bolan and managed to catch the warrior off guard. The blade of his knife sliced through the stretch fabric of Bolan's blacksuit and left a jagged laceration across his chest.

Bolan stepped back quickly, resisting the urge to check the wound. He wasn't dead, but one misstep could make it so he wouldn't have to worry about how bad it was. Seconds ticked off in Bolan's head, and he knew that perhaps thirty seconds remained before Grimaldi put a missile straight into the center of the warehouse and detonated it. The Executioner needed to end this quickly, and he wasn't sure how to do that and still make it out in time. The best he could hope for, in this case, was to stall long enough for Grimaldi to finish the mission.

And it looked to the Executioner like this was where the curtain fell on the final act.

Washington, D.C.

TYRA MACEWAN WAS JOLTED awake by something cold and wet splashed on her face.

She inadvertently inhaled some of the water, and she choked and spit to regurgitate some of the water. This was followed by a fit of coughing before she finally calmed enough to take in her surroundings. The first thing she saw was Malcolm Shurish's grinning visage, standing over her with a triumphant glare and an empty glass. She became conscious of the fact that her hands and feet were tied to a pair of upright columns, and those columns were supporting a low ceiling. There were windows scattered throughout the room at the level of the ceiling, but they were blackened with some type of thick tinting material. It didn't take her long to determine she was in some type of basement.

"Welcome back to the world of the living, my dear," Shurish said, chuckling at her with a sardonic expression. "I am honored to have the pleasure of your company during such an historic moment."

"Go fuck yourself, Malcolm!"

"Now, now," Shurish chided her, wagging his finger and shaking his head. "That is certainly not the language I would expect from any respectable woman of your talent and intelligence. You surprise me."

"Didn't you know, Malcolm?" MacEwan responded with as much distaste as she could muster. "I'm still a good old-fashioned Texas girl. And if I had my six-shooter with me, I'd blow your head clean off."

"Tsk-tsk, such a temper," Shurish replied.

"Definitely not what I would have expected from such a good-looking broad," a stranger's voice said.

Shurish and MacEwan turned with surprise to see a man standing at the base of the steps, his weight balanced precariously on a cane. His hair was almost pure white, as was his complexion, and his eyes were yellow with liver disease. The skin itself was dry, and flakes of it were visible against the expensive, three-piece Armani suit that hung almost robelike on his bony form. Three large men stood around him like giant trees shading and protecting a seedling, and the bulges in their jackets betrayed their entire purpose. MacEwan looked toward Shurish, looking for some sign of recognition, but it wasn't there.

"Don't look so surprised, Dr. Shurish," the man said, followed immediately by a cackling laugh. "We are partners, after all. At least, I thought we were, until I found out you had abandoned poor Rhatib and sent Abdalrahman off on some wild-goose chase. Did you think I wouldn't take whatever steps necessary to protect my investment?"

"But…but…" Shurish stammered, "the alarms and the intruder detection system should have alerted—"

The man waved his hand and said, "Child's play for my technical people. We've been watching this place for weeks. We knew about your little hideout here in the Appalachians." The man made a show of looking at the surroundings, and then continued, "Of course, I prefer something a bit more contemporary and larger, shall we say, but everyone has different tastes."

"I don't know who you are," Shurish said, reaching for a desk drawer near him, "but you had better get out of here!"

"Ah, now, Dr. Shurish, I wouldn't do that," the man said as the three bodyguards suddenly drew weapons. "Surely you know that my men could kill you before you ever got to your own gun. So let's not play childish games. After all, we are still partners and I don't yet think you would have been stupid enough to screw *me* over. Would you have done something like that, Doctor?"

And then, MacEwan saw a look spread across Shurish's face, an expression of realization and unbridled terror. He whispered, "Lenzini."

Nicolas Lenzini smiled. "Correct."

"But you're not—"

"No, I'm not the man you met. That was one of my many body doubles. You see, I'm dying of…well, many things is probably the best way for me to put it. Riotous and gluttonous living has left my body little more than a rotting shell. But I swore I would live long enough to see my empire grow and prosper. And my legacy will be realized by your system as soon as it goes online."

"You will not live to see that system go online," Shurish said. "You have betrayed the New Islamic Front, and they will not let you live once they know you have betrayed them."

"And who is going to be left to tell them, eh, Doctor?" Lenzini said. "Are you planning on exacting retribution against me for the NIF? You don't believe in their cause any more than I do. Poor Malcolm Shurish, an overachiever, poorly mistreated and greatly misunderstood by his government. You didn't honestly believe that I would forge any sort of true alliance with the likes of your people, did you?"

"You set up this entire thing?"

"No, *you* set it up, Dr. Shurish. You and Rhatib, and your silly little terrorist network. I'm simply the one who will control it."

"You can't control it," MacEwan interjected.

"Shut up, bitch!" Lenzini shouted and then succumbed to a violent fit of coughing. He had one of his men help him to a chair while the other two kept Shurish and MacEwan covered with pistols. When he'd settled down, and the coughing had subsided, he continued, "I will deal with you in good time, woman. For now, I would keep your mouth shut! This is a matter among men."

Lenzini returned his attention to Shurish. "So what is it to be, Doctor? Are you going to honor the terms of our arrangement, or do I kill you now?"

"Even if I die, Sadiq will still have total control of the system," Shurish said. "You can kill me, but you will never possess the key to our systems, or to the communications satellite we hid."

"Oh, yes," Lenzini said mockingly, "I forgot to tell you about that. You see, your communications satellite is about to be destroyed. It seems that is a failure on the part of both sides. My men could not kill the man who penetrated our organization, a man named Frankie Lambretta, and neither could Colonel Abdalrahman kill this same man, whose name I believe is Cooper. So, that means your satellite is gone, as is my network. However, I know that you have an alternative program that will still allow us to seize control of the American defense systems at both Norad and the Pentagon. And that will be enough."

"He's talking about Operation Poltergeist, Malcolm," MacEwan said. "He knows about it."

"Oh yes, the woman is right for once," Lenzini added. "We do know about this special code that reassembles data at high speeds and when combined with your programming algorithms it sends a code through the SuperNet systems and reroutes all defense control to one system."

"The system you have right here," MacEwan said quietly, realizing now what Shurish had done to secure his future. Suddenly, she felt the bile rise in her throat and an unspeakable hatred for the man she'd once worked for, a man she had looked up to with unquestioning loyalty and respect. "You're a monster! You're going to let this man manipulate you into destroying your own country! You can go to hell, Malcolm! Do you hear me? You can go to hell!"

And as Shurish stood and stared at her in complete shock, Nicolas Lenzini cackled some more and replied, "He's already there, my dear."

Seattle, Washington

Thirty seconds remained.

Mack Bolan deflected another violent lunge by Abdalrahman. This time, however, the warrior was ready for the counterattack when it came. His opponent dropped to one knee and tried to sweep Bolan's feet out from under him, but the Executioner jumped over the attack. The force of Abdalrahman's movement left him off balance, and Bolan used that to his advantage. He drove his boot upward and caught the terrorist under the chin with the kick while the man was still trying to regain his feet. Abdalrahman let out a cry of pain as blood spewed from his mouth and several teeth broke away.

The terrorist rolled away and came to his feet, his eyes filled with contempt as he studied Bolan beneath his eyebrows. He weaved on unsteady feet and waited for the Executioner to make his next move. Bolan edged forward slashing at the man with his knife. He had no intention of actually executing an attack on the terrorist as much as he did keeping him off balance. Bolan looked in Abdalrahman's eyes and realized that the man who stood before him was a culmination of all the hatred and fanaticism of the New Islamic Front.

Twenty seconds…

"You will not leave here alive," Abdalrahman growled. "It is my destiny to make sure you do not."

"Maybe that's your destiny," Bolan said, "but I make my own."

The warrior stepped forward again, and Abdalrahman took another step backward. He tripped over one of the large clamp-and-bolt mechanisms that stabilized the base framework of the satellite dish. He tried to keep his balance by moving sideways, but it drew his attention and compromised his defensive posture.

Bolan moved on that. The soldier jumped over the framework and fired a rock hard punch to Abdalrahman's head. The man reeled from the blow, twisting and trying to escape, but he was stopped by the crisscrossed pipes and slick metalwork of the monstrous dish. Abdalrahman was seething as he turned and attempted to fight, but Bolan knew he couldn't let up the assault. The soldier launched a side kick to Abdalrahman's solar plexus, driving the air from the man's lungs. Abdalrahman let out a wheeze even as he swung his knife wildly, but Bolan had the upper hand and he easily avoided Abdalrahman's moves of desperation.

Ten seconds…

Abdalrahman screamed with everything he had left and put it into a mad charge at Bolan. The warrior stepped aside and clotheslined the terrorist, and as his adversary fell backward, Bolan drove the Colt Combat Commander knife into the base of his neck. The terrorist's eyes went wide as he took his last breath and his body stopped receiving signals from the brain. His body trembled spasmodically and he collapsed to cold, gray floor of the warehouse.

Three seconds…

The Executioner was moving for the exit, his heart racing and his lungs expanding as his heart pumped life-giving blood to every muscle and cell in his body. He went through the still-open door without breaking stride and emerged onto the pavement. Fires from hot tracer rounds had engulfed several of the nearby buildings, and the NIF terrorists were running around in disorganized fashion as the Learjet passed overhead and spit another violent storm of rounds at them.

Bolan keyed up his headset just in time to hear Grimaldi quietly say, "It's away, Sarge, and I sure as hell hope you're clear."

The Executioner was perhaps twenty-five or thirty yards from the warehouse when he heard the first AGM-130 crash through the roof. He knew the safety distance from the blast radius and he also knew he couldn't possibly hope to make it out alive. Still, he wasn't about to give up on the idea. His legs screamed in painful protest as he continued to sprint for the fence line. Bolan reached the corner where he'd first entered and ignored the wire that sliced through his blacksuit and cut into tender flesh as he dived through it. He rolled out of the dive and came to his feet in continuous forward motion.

The warrior suddenly felt the marshy grasslands and the cold splashing of water and in a harrying moment of sheer survival instinct, he threw himself into the thickening grasses and pressed his body as close as he could to the swampy terrain, facedown in the water, hands over his head.

The vibration of the explosion rumbled through the ground and even in his position Bolan could imagine the sight. The flame from the missile would climb to a height of a hundred yards or better, and turn anything within half a city block's radius into molten slag. Bolan could feel the sudden, intense heat on his back, but he knew it wasn't hot enough to cause injuries from that distance. The aftermath of the explosion would rain dust and debris and carry it in the winds for hours. Still, the mission had been accomplished and the Executioner had once more made it out alive.

Yeah, he'd made it!

As Bolan pulled his face and then the rest of his body from the icy mud and water with a sucking noise, he could hear something very faintly—a voice calling from somewhere—a familiar voice calling almost plaintively. Bolan stood wearily and wiped the mud and grass as best he could from this eyes and mouth. What was it? Where was it coming from? The area around him was quiet—deathly quiet—and almost surreal. Then Bolan realized that the receiver of his radio had partially dislodged from his ear, and the voice he heard wasn't a distant voice, but simply a faint one.

Bolan reinserted the earpiece. "Eagle One to Striker, I say again—do you copy, over?"

"Eagle, this is Striker," Bolan replied. "I'm all clear. See you at the rendezvous."

And Jack Grimaldi simply laughed.

Stony Man Farm, Virginia

"MISSION ACCOMPLISHED, boss," Carl Lyons told Brognola over the speakerphone.

His words raised cheers of relief from Harold Brognola, as well as Price, Kurtzman and Kissinger, who were also present to hear the announcement.

"Nice job, Ironman," Brognola said, and since the Stony Man chief rarely used the nickname, everyone knew he meant it. "Rhatib's alive, correct?"

"Roger that," Lyons said. "He wasn't stupid enough to put up a fight. We had a time getting inside their base at the wharf, but it was nothing we haven't seen before. All terrorists were either killed or captured, and we took Rhatib alive, along with all of the equipment he was using."

"What about MacEwan?" Kurtzman asked. "Did you find Tyra MacEwan?"

There was a long pause before Lyons replied, and everyone in the room knew what the answer would be. "No, I'm sorry, Bear. No sign of her."

"Well, let's not jump to conclusions. She could still be alive."

"What about Striker?" Lyons asked. "Any word from him or Jack?"

"They're on their way back," Brognola replied.

Lyons's sigh of relief was audible over the speakers.

Brognola continued, "It seems there was a major communications network in Seattle, and it was primed and ready for action. Striker says he thinks they were able to take it out of action before anything could be done with it, and the White House has confirmed that aside from a few glitches here and there, all defense systems are operating normally and remain fully under our control."

"Well, we, ah, how do I put it?" Lyons replied. "Let's just say we *convinced* this Rhatib character that it was in his best interests to provide us as much information as he could. He told us that Shurish was involved with the operation, and that they were originally working out of a temporary location beneath a house he has somewhere in the Appalachians."

"That wouldn't be far from here," Brognola replied.

"That's exactly what we were thinking."

"What do you want to do?"

"Well, we were only able to get a general location from Rhatib, but it's a narrow enough grid that if Bear could locate it, we might be able to get to this failsafe system and stop it in time."

Price nodded her agreement with the plan. "And if our theory is correct about Shurish being responsible for luring MacEwan into a trap, we might be able to pull her out of the frying pan, as well."

"I think you're both right," Brognola replied. "We'll get back to you on this, Carl. In the meantime, your number-one priority is to insure the secure transfer of Rhatib to federal custody. All other mission objectives are secondary."

Brognola could tell the Able Team leader wasn't happy to hear that sort of order, but he knew the team would do their job with all the efficiency and professionalism he'd come to expect. "Roger that, Chief. Able Team out here."

Brognola aimed a level stare at Kurtzman. His tone was grim, but he tried to remain optimistic as he said, "Bear, it's up to you now."

Kurtzman nodded. "No pressure, though, right?"

"You'll make it happen, Aaron," Price said, putting a hand on his arm and showing him a confident smile. "You're the best we have, and you'll come through."

And with that, Aaron "The Bear" Kurtzman turned to the keyboard and began working his own unique brand of magic.

"WE THINK WE'VE FOUND Shurish's little retreat," Brognola told the Executioner. "Aaron's sending the grid coordinates now by secured uplink to Jack."

"What do you know about it?" Bolan asked.

It was Barbara Price who answered, "It's a large hideaway in the foothills of the Appalachians, about forty miles inside the Monongahela National Forest. It overlooks Lake Moomaw."

"I know the place," Bolan replied. "I've done plenty of hiking and camping through there. It's quiet and out of the way, and it would be the perfect place for Shurish to set up a freestanding system that didn't require any outside support."

"I was going to send Able to check it out," Brognola told him, "but they're still tied up with the transfer of Rhatib. I told them that's the priority, and I don't know how much time we have left."

"I'd have them stick with that, Hal. That's the best use of resources. Jack's reviewed the coordinates, and he's advising that we're less than thirty minutes from the area. I'll take care of this."

"Striker, be careful," Price said. Bolan could hear the concern in her voice. "Shurish is by no means stupid, and we don't want to underestimate him."

"I hear you," Bolan said. "I'll be watchful. Out here."

The Executioner removed the headset, lightly punched Grimaldi on the shoulder with a grin and moved into the back of the plane to prepare for the operation. It was only a matter of time before Shurish got his own system up and running, and Bolan was a little surprised he hadn't already implemented the failsafe. According to the information Able Team had drawn out of Rhatib, and passed through Brognola, Shurish had set up a temporary operation at the target location, but then moved the operations back to Washington, D.C. That didn't make much sense, unless Shurish had something to hide. Well, if he was working out of this new location, and had some backup plan, Bolan would find out about it soon enough.

The other troubling factor was the news about Lenzini's disappearance. The Mafia crime lord had managed to evade the FBI tails arranged by Brognola and Leo Turrin by using one of his body doubles. Bolan couldn't really blame them, though, since they didn't know what Lenzini really looked like. Brognola had arranged, through his DOJ contacts, to convince federal prosecutors to strike a bargain with Serge Grano and his crew—both for their culpability in Lenzini's numbers rackets as well as their stalking of a federal scientist—and so that would probably provide enough information to topple what was left of Lenzini's operations in a number of areas. But Lenzini himself was unaccounted for.

Bolan would deal with him eventually, but now it was time to pull out all of the stops and deliver the final blow. The Executioner could only hope he'd find Tyra MacEwan alive.

And if she wasn't, Malcolm Shurish and anyone else responsible for her death would pay with their lives.

At the signal from Grimaldi, Bolan was out of the plane. The plan had called for a low-level jump of one thousand feet above Lake Moomaw. The coordinates indicated that Shurish's retreat was about a quarter mile off the lake, and hidden well from air observation by the natural greenery and mountainous woodlands of the Monongahela. The lake wasn't frozen solid, but the ice was thick and coarse enough to provide a semidecent parachute landing. As the chute collapsed, the wind carried Bolan, his boots sliding across the ice while the chute acted as a makeshift sail. When the Executioner was about fifty feet from the shoreline, he slapped the quick releases and the parachute disengaged from the harness. Bolan's momentum slowed and by the time he hit shore he was walking under his own power.

The warrior dumped the chute pack and harness, and proceeded toward the location of the cabin. He was armed only with the Beretta and the Desert Eagle, but he was confident that would be enough. It was unlikely that Shurish would have any of the NIF terrorists actually accompanying him—it sounded as if the majority of them had gone down in Able Team's raid at the wharf.

Bolan moved through the woods, glancing occasionally at the gloomy, darkening sky overhead. He was running out of light, and that meant a full-court press to get to the location where they hoped Shurish was holed up. Almost half an hour elapsed before Bolan came upon a clearing and spotted the cabin. Actually, it was a bit more than a cabin. The home—probably paid for by whatever blood money Shurish had accepted from the NIF—was a single story log-cabin style, with a packed gravel drive that appeared to lead to an access road. There was a shiny limousine parked in the drive, positioned immediately behind a luxury sedan.

The Executioner checked the perimeter for security and took quick notice of a small box that looked as if it housed an electric eye. Bolan moved to the box and placed one hand on it. There was no heat and no exterior exposures indicating it was wired to blow if molested. He located an access panel on the side and flipped it open to find the wires inside had been cut cleanly in two. Somebody had already neutralized the security system. That concerned Bolan, since it meant that Shurish had other enemies, enemies that were possibly inside.

Bolan loosed the Beretta, thumbed the selector to single shot and kept low as he advanced on the house. He reached the porch steps unchallenged, ascended them and catfooted his way to the front door. The screen door was unlocked, and a careful twist of the doorknob produced a soft click. The door moved inward and Bolan slipped inside. He went low, bracing his shoulder against one wall of the foyer, and tracked the room with the muzzle of his pistol. All was quiet, and then he heard voices.

Bolan took a deep breath and steeled his nerves, willing himself to an almost meditative state. He closed his eyes for a moment, turned his ear in the direction of the voices, then got to his feet and moved with stealth to a closed door five feet away. With the exception of a hallway light, the rest of the house was dark and gloomy. Shadows in the outside twilight played across the floors, and Bolan could feel a sense of foreboding creep over his skin and settle at the base of his neck.

A small glow spilled from under the closed door. Bolan turned the handle and opened it just enough to gain a view of a descending stairwell: a basement. He opened the door a little more and pushed the Beretta ahead of him. His sights came to rest on a big, hulking figure with his back toward the Executioner. He was dressed in a tailored suit and in his hand Bolan saw a large pistol. Bolan could only see part of the man's face, and a quick search of his mental files told him the face was familiar. He couldn't immediately place the mug, and then it dawned on him. He'd seen this guy inside the home of Nicolas Lenzini.

That explained the limo, and it also explained a hell of a lot more. Lenzini had forged some type of alliance with Malcolm Shurish, and whatever they had planned certainly wasn't good. Kurtzman had reported some unusual electronic signatures coming from the area, and there was definite activity inside Lenzini's network, even after the destruction of the satellite dish. Still, Bolan couldn't understand it—he'd neutralized that system. They had shut down every major component and closed every hole. That could only mean that Shurish had masterminded a backup if all else failed, and proved MacEwan's theory that only an exit code entered at the source would shut it down now and forever.

Bolan opened the door and leveled his sights on the Mafia gunman's head as he descended the stairs. The Executioner triggered the weapon on the run. The 135-grain semijacketed hollowpoint round punched through the hard guy's skull and pitched his body onto a flimsy table. The table collapsed under the man's weight and rained books, glasses and a pile of other debris onto the corpse as it hit the ground.

Bolan reached the bottom of the steps and pegged two more hostiles. One of the mobsters was clawing for gun leather when the Executioner's first shot caught him through the hand. The man pulled his arm free, his pistol clattering to the floor from beneath his jacket, the bones in the hand shattered and exposed. The man screamed as blood began to spurt uncontrollably in various directions. Bolan's second round went straight through his gaping mouth and blew out the back of his head.

The Executioner shoulder rolled past a couch where Lenzini was seated. The old man was screaming and coughing, obviously choking on his own saliva as he ordered the remaining bull to end the carnage. The Mafia soldier started firing, but he hadn't been selective of his targets, and while his rounds found their mark it was not the correct one. Two of the .45-caliber bullets from the shooter's pistol crashed through Lenzini's chest, and the crime boss's screams died in his throat, replaced by blood and lung tissue.

Bolan came to one knee, braced his forearms across the back of the couch and steadied the pistol in a Weaver's grip. The warrior unleashed a 3-round volley. The first round connected with the enemy gunman's pistol hand, smashing bones and vital tissue and sending the pistol skittering across the floor. The remaining pair of 9 mm slugs punched through his skull, the first splitting his head open while the second did more of the same. The man's nearly headless corpse staggered backward and connected with a support beam before collapsing to the concrete.

The Executioner stood and tracked the room before he settled on Shurish's quivering form—the guy was cowering in a corner. Fearful sobs emanated from him, and Bolan's finger eased off the trigger. The warrior kept his pistol pointed at Shurish, but his eyes flicked to MacEwan and studied her with a practiced stare of concern. She didn't look any worse for the wear.

"It's about time, Cooper," she said.

"I got a little sidetracked," he growled. "You okay?"

"Yeah, but the rest of the country won't be if you don't cut me loose."

"What's going on?" he asked as he moved over to her and untied her bonds.

She didn't answer him until he had her untied. She rubbed her hands and rushed to a nearby computer terminal. "He's activated the code to assemble the programs."

Bolan whirled and pointed the pistol at Shurish's forehead. "Stop it, or I'll kill you here and now."

"I didn't want to do it," Shurish cried. "I really didn't want to do it! Lenzini made me start the sequence. I wasn't going—"

"Quit stalling and tell us how to stop it!"

Shurish locked glances with MacEwan, who sat at the keyboard and waited expectantly for him to say something. "You have to wait until the precise moment. If you start the abort sequence before recompilations are complete, the program will lock you out of the system, and—"

"Is there an exit code?" MacEwan screamed at him.

"Yes," he whispered.

"Give it to her," Bolan commanded him.

Shurish began to give the instructions to her, and while Bolan barely understood a word of it, MacEwan was nodding in unison with his instructions. She began to type furiously, moving between keyboards and entering characters and digits at a furious pace. Numbers and letters echoed back to her on the screens, and Bolan watched with fascination as her eyes scanned multiple lines of code that seemed to be moving across the terminal windows faster than any normal human being could have possibly hoped to read them. Still, it seemed like it made perfect sense to MacEwan.

Finally, she said, "All right, we're inside the system but we're going to have to hook into Bear's network in order to distribute the information across the SuperNet."

Bolan went to the phone, dialed the direct emergency number and handed the receiver to MacEwan. She quickly explained the situation and then nodded as Kurtzman obviously began to act on the information. She spit numbers and letters at him, going on continuously about IP addresses and subnet masks and gateway identifiers. A few minutes later, the mask of concentration was broken.

MacEwan looked at Bolan, and with a wink and a cocksure grin she said, "There you go, Cooper. Nothing but Net."

And the Executioner laughed.

Epilogue

Now this is more like it, Jack Grimaldi thought.

The Stony Man pilot looked out from the porch and studied the breathtaking views of the ranch. Tyra MacEwan's home was nice, to say the least, but nothing could beat these kinds of views. The flier had decided to take some time off and he couldn't think of anything better than spending that R&R with a beautiful and intelligent woman. Something had ignited a spark between Grimaldi and the gutsy, old-fashioned woman from Amarillo, and while he knew it wouldn't last, he was comfortable with it in the here and now.

MacEwan knew it as well; she knew there were reasons such a relationship couldn't be permanent. Nonetheless, it didn't stop them from enjoying a bit of time together, and he wondered what she was thinking even as they sat on the porch swing and rocked while she rested her head on his shoulder. Both had wounds that needed mending, internal and external, but that was okay. Grimaldi would go back to his job, eventually, and she would go back to hers, and that was probably the last they would ever see of each other.

Still, it didn't mean they couldn't be together for right now.

"How are you feeling?" MacEwan asked.

"I'm okay," he said. "I think I'm feeling much better now that I'm here with you."

"I hate to bring it up," she said, raising her head from his shoulder and looking at him.

He saw the sparkling mischief in her eyes. "What?" he asked.

"I was wondering how Cooper was doing?" She shook her head, laughed lightly and added. "No, wait. What is it you call him? 'The Sarge'?"

Grimaldi couldn't resist a sheepish grin. "Yeah, the Sarge."

"Have you spoken with him?"

"No, not since he left for parts unknown."

"You two have a strange relationship," she stated. "You know that, don't you?"

"It's crossed my mind once or twice," Grimaldi replied easily. "But I owe that guy. You have no idea how much I owe that guy."

"What happened?"

"I can't talk about it, Tyra," Grimaldi said. "You know that."

"Yes," she whispered, settling her head back on his shoulder and snuggling against him. "I guess I do."

"Just suffice it to say that I wouldn't be alive today if it weren't for him." Grimaldi smiled, although he knew Mac-Ewan couldn't see it, and he thought of another time. A time long, long ago in a city called Las Vegas.

"Where do you think he's gone to?"

Grimaldi sighed. "Not a clue. But you can bet wherever it is that it's where he's most needed."

"Doesn't that guy ever slow down?"

"This would be a much harsher and dangerous world if he slowed down. But that's his way. He knows what he's doing, and he does it extremely well. He's a far better man than any I've known, Tyra. And he's done far greater things than most men could ever hope to do. That's just who he is. It's what *makes* him who he is. Do you understand?"

"Not entirely, I suppose," she replied with a deep sigh. "But then it doesn't really matter. I guess the important thing is that he's out there risking his life so that all of us can have better ones."

"You do understand," Grimaldi replied. "And wherever you go or whatever you do, the best thing in the world you can do for him is to remember that."

And as they sat together and watched the sun set, Jack Grimaldi did just that.

He remembered.

Readers won't want to miss
this exciting new title
of the SuperBolan series!

Point of Betrayal

The fallout of a Middle East conspiracy could spell
disaster for America.

A soldier from Iraq's toppled regime is back for
blood and glory, ready to light the fuse that will
deliver a killing blow to the Middle East—but it's
the United States that will take the ultimate fall.
Up against traitors, terrorists and impossible odds,
Mack Bolan races to pull America's future out of
the crosshairs of a violent enemy.

*Available September 2005
at your favorite retailer.*

Or order your copy now by sending your name, address, zip or postal code, along with a check or
money order (please do not send cash) for $6.50 for each book ordered ($7.99 in Canada), plus
75¢ postage and handling ($1.00 in Canada), payable to Gold Eagle Books, to:

In the U.S.	In Canada
Gold Eagle Books	Gold Eagle Books
3010 Walden Avenue	P.O. Box 636
P.O. Box 9077	Fort Erie, Ontario
Buffalo, NY 14269-9077	L2A 5X3

Please specify book title with your order.
Canadian residents add applicable federal and provincial taxes.

GOLD
EAGLE®

GSB104

DEATHLANDS · EXECUTIONER · SUPER BOLAN · OUTLANDERS · DESTROYER · STONY MAN

FREE

SCREENSAVERS
CELLPHONE RINGS
E-POSTCARDS
GAMES
and much much more...

Available at
www.cuttingaudio.com

DEATHLANDS · EXECUTIONER · SUPER BOLAN · OUTLANDERS · DESTROYER · STONY MAN

GECCGEN05MM

TAKE 'EM FREE
2 action-packed novels plus a mystery bonus
NO RISK
NO OBLIGATION TO BUY

SPECIAL LIMITED-TIME OFFER

Mail to: Gold Eagle Reader Service™

IN U.S.A.:
3010 Walden Ave.
P.O. Box 1867
Buffalo, NY 14240-1867

IN CANADA:
P.O. Box 609
Fort Erie, Ontario
L2A 5X3

YEAH! Rush me 2 FREE Gold Eagle® novels and my FREE mystery bonus. If I don't cancel, I will receive 6 hot-off-the-press novels every other month. Bill me at the low price of just $29.94* for each shipment. That's a savings of over 10% off the combined cover prices and there is NO extra charge for shipping and handling! There is no minimum number of books I must buy. I can always cancel at any time simply by returning a shipment at your cost or by returning any shipping statement marked "cancel." Even if I never buy another book from Gold Eagle, the 2 free books and mystery bonus are mine to keep forever.

166 ADN DZ76
366 ADN DZ77

Name _____ (PLEASE PRINT)

Address _____ Apt. No. _____

City _____ State/Prov. _____ Zip/Postal Code _____

Signature (if under 18, parent or guardian must sign)

Not valid to present Gold Eagle® subscribers.
Want to try two free books from another series? Call 1-800-873-8635.

* Terms and prices subject to change without notice. Sales tax applicable in N.Y. Canadian residents will be charged applicable provincial taxes and GST. This offer is limited to one order per household. All orders subject to approval.
® are trademarks owned and used by the trademark owner and or its licensee.
© 2004 Harlequin Enterprises Ltd.

GE-04R

MAELSTROM

The fuse of a new global war is lit on America's streets....

An advanced weapon prototype is hijacked by an unidentified group of mercenaries and followed by a wave of massacres in the streets of America's cities. The torch of anarchy and hatred has been lit, and waves of destruction have begun to spread across the globe. A crisis has erupted as angry radicals are poised to become deadly freedom fighters so powerful that not even the superpowers can oppose them. Stony Man's only chance...America's only chance...is to strike first, strike hard, strike now....

STONY MAN®

*Available
August 2005
at your favorite retailer.*

Or order your copy now by sending your name, address, zip or postal code, along with a check or money order (please do not send cash) for $6.50 for each book ordered ($7.99 in Canada), plus 75¢ postage and handling ($1.00 in Canada), payable to Gold Eagle Books, to:

In the U.S.

Gold Eagle Books
3010 Walden Avenue
P.O. Box 9077
Buffalo, NY 14269-9077

In Canada

Gold Eagle Books
P.O. Box 636
Fort Erie, Ontario
L2A 5X3

Please specify book title with your order.
Canadian residents add applicable federal and provincial taxes.

GOLD EAGLE®

GSM78

James Axler
Outlanders®

SUCCESSORS
PLAGUE OF DEMONS

Two centuries after a nuclear holocaust, America continues to resurrect itself, survival being the primary impulse for the hammered masses, while absolute power remains in the hands of the reborn barons and their Magistrate enforcer corps.

Thawed from cryogenic stasis, Gilgamesh Bates is a twentieth-century madman with enough knowledge of preDark secrets to create a new world order. To inherit the earth, he's unleashed an ecological plague in the middle of the Amazon—a bioengineered contagion from which there is no escape.

Available August 2005 at your favorite retailer.

Or order your copy now by sending your name, address, zip or postal code, along with a check or money order (please do not send cash) for $6.50 for each book ordered ($7.99 in Canada), plus 75¢ postage and handling ($1.00 in Canada), payable to Gold Eagle Books, to:

In the U.S.	In Canada
Gold Eagle Books	Gold Eagle Books
3010 Walden Avenue	P.O. Box 636
P.O. Box 9077	Fort Erie, Ontario
Buffalo, NY 14269-9077	L2A 5X3

Please specify book title with your order.
Canadian residents add applicable federal and provincial taxes.

GOLD EAGLE®

GOUT34